Adam's Ambition

Emerald Springs Legacy Book One

MONICA TILLERY
author of *Kiss Me, Katie*

CRIMSON
ROMANCE

F+W Media, Inc.

Published by
Crimson Romance
an imprint of F+W Media, Inc.
10151 Carver Road, Suite 200
Blue Ash, OH 45242. U.S.A.
www.crimsonromance.com

ISBN 10: 1-4405-7097-3
ISBN 13: 978-1-4405-7097-1
eISBN 10: 1-4405-7098-1
eISBN 13: 978-1-4405-7098-8

Cover art © 123rf.com; iStockphoto.com/kevin miller; GlobalStock.

For Lisa Gill, Jill Hill, Leslie McKinney,
Lydia Schultz, and Amy Valentine.

Everything is better with great friends,
and y'all are some of the best.

Acknowledgments

Adam's Ambition is the first book in Crimson Romance's first continuity, the Emerald Springs Legacy. Four more books by four authors will come after it to carry on the story of Emerald Springs's families, and the process has been unlike anything I've ever experienced before. I have had the best time working on this series, and I am honored to be included with such talented authors. Working out storylines to span five books, keeping everything uniform throughout the series, and cackling behind the scenes about our characters' antics has been crazy fun and truly such a joy.

My heartfelt thanks to Nicole Flockton, who had a crazy idea one night about pitching a continuity to Crimson Romance ... and was kind enough to let me tag along. To Holley Trent, who always makes me laugh and writes the best dialogue. To Elley Arden, who has it together in a way that makes me want to be her when I grow up and is a lovely person I wish I lived closer to. And to Robyn Neeley, who writes sweet romantic comedy like nobody's business and took on the supremely difficult task of tying up all these loose ends in the last book. Working with you girls makes me wish all my books could be written with a group of friends. I'd love to do it again.

Julie Sturgeon, you have the patience of a saint and the editorial eyes of an eagle. Thank you so much for the thorough and insightful editing, which made *Adam's Ambition* a book we can be proud of. Working with you has been such a pleasure, and I'd love to do it again.

I'd especially like to thank Jennifer Lawler, who saw the value in this series and signed me on, even though I was a new author with little experience. I remember the rush of excitement I felt when it all started coming together, and I'll never forget it.

Chapter One

Adam Whitman twirled his favorite Mont Blanc Starwalker in his fingers, enjoying the weight, and smiled to himself. This deal and the promotion that went along with it were as good as his. The partnership between Eco Initiatives and Everlight Optics would be the biggest contract he or anyone else at the company had ever brokered, and if he could just get the woman across from his desk to sign on the dotted line, it would be done.

"You're telling me you were a farmer? As in, you were out there in the field, picking tea leaves?" Christine Grazioli, Everlight Optic's CEO, shot him a suggestive smile from her spot on the sofa in his office.

He'd seen that look before, and if he played his cards right, the ink would be dry on the contract by noon. "I certainly did, from the time I could walk until the day I left home. My family owns the largest tea farm in Washington. You've probably had some yourself. Hold out your hand." He paused and picked up a crystal bowl on the table, holding it out to her. "Pick one."

She plucked a leaf from the bowl and handed it to him. He gave her a conspiratorial smile and turned the leaf over in his hand. "Nice choice. It says that an important decision you make will bring you much success." He dropped the leaf above her hand, letting it float gently into her open palm.

Christine laughed, throaty and seductive. "I don't think that's how tea leaf reading works. You're supposed to brew these and read what's left behind after I drink the tea." She glanced at her watch. "Oh, shoot. I've lost track of time. I need to get across town for a meeting at Paramount. Can we get in touch later?"

"Absolutely. I'll have the contract sent to your office; just send it back when you've reviewed everything and signed." He stood and opened the door. Once his client was safely down the hall, Adam fist-pumped the air in silent celebration. All it took was a nice working lunch and some harmless flirting, and he was on his way to closing a six-figure deal and locking in the promotion. This partnership would make the Eco Initiatives higher-ups very happy and guarantee him one fat end-of-year bonus. He laughed to himself; sometimes it was too easy. The tea leaves always did the trick. Women either believed in the magic or allowed themselves to think there was something between them. Who would have thought his upbringing on the family tea farm would still come in handy? He returned to his desk to review the paperwork so he'd be ready when she sealed the deal.

"Mr. Whitman, Richard Whitman is on line one." His assistant's disembodied voice came through the phone speaker, and he looked up from the proposal. How long had it been since he spoke with his father? Weeks at least. Far too long.

"Thank you, Lauren." Adam pressed a button on his phone and answered the call. "Hi, Dad." He sat back in his chair and relaxed, ready for a long chat. The deal with Everlight Optics would still be there when he finished with his family. He hadn't given them enough time lately. Or for the last several years, if he were to be honest with himself.

"Hey, son. Is now a good time?" The voice came through the line robust and hearty. It was good to hear him sounding so upbeat. They exchanged pleasantries until his father reached the real reason for his call. "I need you to come home."

Adam sat up straight. "What's wrong?" Fear gripped him and his blood ran icy in his veins. His father had asked him to come home once before, and only once. That time his mother's illness was taking a turn for the worse, and he had barely made it in time to say his goodbyes before she passed away.

His dad laughed. "Relax. Nothing's wrong. I'm looking to retire, and I could really use your help. Do you think you could get away for a week or two?"

A week or two? He would be lucky to make it through the weekend without getting a call about something. His job at Eco Initiatives left little time for any semblance of a normal life. When he wasn't busy with his own accounts, he was consulting on others or researching the latest technological advances in environmental sciences. His days were spent helping local L.A. businesses green their operations through technological improvements, training company sustainability officers, and consulting for lobby groups. He enjoyed working for Eco Initiatives so much, he rarely took vacation days and regularly worked sixty-hour weeks. Still, losing his mother taught him that he'd regret squandering his time when his family needed him. Once someone was gone, they were gone forever. If his father was asking him to come home, Adam knew better than to second-guess it. He never wanted to look back and wish he'd chosen differently.

"I could come up for a few days, probably. I don't know about a week." If his hunch was correct, his father wanted him to consider taking over the farm. His father had made no secret of the fact he wanted his eldest son to claim his place at the head of the family business, Emerald Tea Farm, to live out his legacy. He had heard it all his life and had resisted the pressure. His dad was getting older, and with no replacement in line, it might be more difficult to work it out this time. There was no chance that could be managed in a week.

"Adam, I need you, and I don't think we can wrap it up in a few days. I want to settle everything while I'm still able. I don't want to end up with a situation where I'm forced to hand everything over to the first willing body because I'm too old to do anything about it. Now will you come help me or not?" His voice was strong, determined.

"What about Chad and Daniel? What do they have to say about all this?" His younger brothers still lived in Emerald Springs and ran the family's other businesses. They would never come out and say it, but he always suspected they resented the assumption he would take over the farm, the family's lifeblood, when he was the one who left. Chad and Daniel remained loyal to the family in ways he simply hadn't, and they likely wondered why their father wanted Adam to come home so badly.

"Chad is busy with the restaurant, and Daniel has his hands full with the resort. They both say they're willing to help with the farm, but honestly I don't think either one of them has the time for it. They'd let the whole thing run into the ground before they'd admit they're not up for the job."

He laughed. His father was right; they would drop from exhaustion before they would ask him for help. "That's true, but what makes you think it'll do any good for me to be there?"

"Maybe you can talk some sense into them and help them realize they need to leave it to someone else, or maybe you'll come up with some way they can juggle everything. We might end up hiring someone to oversee operations, someone who doesn't have other businesses to worry about. That can only happen after we let the boys decide they can't do it, though. They'll never accept someone else if they don't get their fair shake first. Who knows? You might finally decide to join the family business."

His father rarely brought up the possibility of hiring an outsider to take over, and Adam took notice. If they were addressing the matter directly, Dad might finally be ready to retire for real—and had given up on Adam taking his place. He was surprised to feel the first twinges of disappointment and quickly dismissed them. He didn't want the farm. He had spent his entire childhood dreaming of leaving town and never picking tea again. He should welcome his father finally moving on, so why did it feel like something was being taken from him?

"I haven't worked in the fields in years, Dad. I don't know how much good I could do," Adam stalled.

"You know how little actual farming I do nowadays, right?" He could hear the smile in his father's voice. "I'm not exactly out picking tea."

"Yeah, I guess I can't remember the last time you really got your hands dirty." He sat back in his chair and stretched. "All right, Dad. I haven't taken vacation time in a while, and I suppose I can always work online if anything urgent comes up. I'll be there. I can probably swing five or six days." He clicked his mouse and scanned the calendar on his computer to be sure nothing pressing would keep him from visiting Emerald Springs.

"Thank you. This means a lot to me." Relief colored his father's tone.

"It's no big deal. Just give me a couple of days to get ready, and I'll be there. I'll let you know when I have a flight to Washington."

They ended the call, and he tapped his pen on his desk blotter, mentally calculating how much time he'd need before he could leave town with a relatively clear work schedule. The sooner he went to Emerald Springs and got everything squared away, the better. The nagging thought that his life wasn't tied up as neatly as he thought ate away at his confidence.

Over the past fifteen years, he'd held out hope his brothers would manage to work together to keep the farm in the family, but the other Whitman enterprises must be commanding too much of their attention. Daniel had always preferred the family resort, a perfect match for his attention to detail and appreciation for luxury, although Chad's work at the family restaurant was surprising, given that he excelled at the art of dodging responsibility. Adam had known tea farming since he could walk, and now he was in the position to take the company to another level. The farm had always been all-organic, but Richard couldn't fracture his focus enough to commit fully to both optimal farming and green operations. Adam could come in with fifteen years of education and experience and a fresh perspective, ready to revolutionize things.

He didn't actually want to leave his life and job in L.A., but now that he had time to dissect their conversation, Adam wondered why his father hadn't tried again to convince him to come aboard? It was probably best this way, best that his family held no unrealistic hopes or expectations of him. This way he could go home for a brief stay, do his part then get back to his life. So why did it feel like he was trying to convince himself? Could it be a small part of him longed for the life he always felt destined to live? No, surely not. He had worked tirelessly to create his new life; there was no way he longed for a return to the farm.

A senior partner stepped in from the hallway and rapped his knuckles on the doorjamb, interrupting his thoughts.

"Hey, Adam, you got a minute?" he asked.

He shut the browser window on his computer and stood, straightening his tie. "Sure, Mr. Campbell. Come on in. Can I get you a coffee or water?"

"Call me Mark, and no thank you, I'm fine. Please, sit." The partner came in and took a seat opposite him.

Adam sat but didn't relax as he waited for Mark to speak. He tried for an expression that said he was loose but confident. "I wanted to talk with you about your future at Eco Initiatives today. We've been watching you for a while, and you have an excellent record here. You're innovative, personable, and efficient. We appreciate your commitment to the environment and to the clients, and we feel that nobody else would be better suited for the position of accounts management for all of California."

He leaned back, ran his fingers through his hair, and blew out a long breath. "Wow. This is quite a surprise."

Mark laughed. "It shouldn't be. You've worked hard, and we think you're ready for the next level. Of course it comes with a lot more responsibility, but the compensation package will reflect that."

"I am flattered, really. This is an amazing opportunity. Would you give me a little while to think it over?" With this promotion, his dream job really, so close within his grasp, Emerald Springs seemed miles away. Strange how things could change so drastically. Just moments ago, he had almost allowed himself to consider taking over the farm.

Mark put his foot back on the floor and looked Adam in the eye. "Sure, of course. Take your time. I'll send over the details so you can see what you'd be getting yourself into, and you let me know what you think."

Adam stood as Mark did, and they shook hands. "Thank you, sir. I appreciate your faith in me."

"You earned it." Mark left, and Adam paced the length of his office, jingling change in his pocket, shocked by the news.

Chapter Two

Adam rented a car once he landed at Sea-Tac—it was better to maintain a bit of freedom during his visit than be at the mercy of his family to drive him around. The more he depended on them during his stay, the harder it would be to disentangle himself from Emerald Tea Farm. His life was in L.A., not here. The fact he continually reminded himself of this didn't escape his notice, but he would tuck that away for later. He would drive in, help his father figure out the best way to handle his retirement, and drive out. He could catch up with the family and enjoy the visit, but he wouldn't get caught up in their lives, and he wouldn't stay any longer than he had to. He'd spent his high school years wishing he could be his own person, not just another Whitman boy. Getting snared by the town and family name again would mean that his years away hadn't done any good.

...

Springtime in the Pacific Northwest was absolutely breathtaking in its beauty, something Adam tended to forget after spending so many years in the city. As he drove into Emerald Springs, the air became sweeter, lighter, and everything was cleaner. It was refreshing to drive through areas with more land than people, to get away from L.A.'s hectic congestion. He flew past fields of green stretching out across the landscape, lush flower gardens, and farms both large and small. For someone so committed to good environmental stewardship, he certainly didn't spend much time in nature. All the green initiatives he designed for companies were launched from within the confines of conference rooms and the occasional employee retreat. Between hunching over plans and being stuck in meetings, he was lucky if he could even take his lunch break outside.

Emerald Springs had changed since he'd left for college, but so much of it was the same. Homes and businesses had sprung up like mushrooms after a rainfall, yet many of the neighboring farms and familiar establishments from his youth were still standing right where he left them. He turned down the road to his family's farm and rolled down the windows, letting the fresh air and his last moments of peace wash over him. He loved his father and brothers fiercely but had come to prefer the solitary order of his life in L.A. There, he was a competent businessman, someone who solved problems and made the world a better place. There, he wasn't the oldest Whitman kid, the one who'd wrecked his dad's tractor when he was ten years old, or the one who got so muddy during a fight with his brothers that his mother wouldn't let him in the house before she sprayed him down with the water hose. He wasn't the one who broke the heart of the only girl he'd ever loved.

The more distance between him and the farm, the better. That way, it was easier to forget the pain he'd caused.

He passed the farm where his childhood home sat at the front of acres upon acres of green fields of tea. No one had lived in that house for several years. Now, his father lived in town and had converted much of the home to usable office space. The master bedroom remained ready for use on those nights when Richard stayed at the farm late or when out-of-town visitors needed somewhere to sleep. The big difference, the one nobody mentioned, was that the bed in that space was new. Adam's mother had spent long hours in their old bed, wanting to be close to Richard when he worked but unable to sit up for long periods of time toward the end of her life. When she passed away, Richard erased all traces of her illness from the house, preferring instead to remember her as the beautiful, vibrant woman he married.

The farm had grown so much, it scarcely resembled the place Adam remembered; in his youth, his father and the three boys tended the fields, developing their love of nature and forging bonds of brotherhood that years and miles couldn't break. Now, the business required a fleet of workers to keep everything running smoothly. Acres flew by as he drove on, until Split Acres Farm came into view. His father's former partner, Joe Sanders, started it as his own place when they dissolved their relationship twenty years ago, and Joe had struggled ever since. Even in L.A., Adam heard of the troubles facing the Sanders place.

As he navigated through town, Adam felt the stirrings of nostalgia. Everything in L.A. was so sophisticated and jaded compared to life in his hometown. Coming home was hard on his conscience, but it soothed him in a way nothing else could. He turned down his radio and rolled up the windows as he pulled into his father's neighborhood, surprised to find his heart pounding in anticipation of reuniting with the family.

He parked in the driveway and pulled his bags from the trunk. Lugging the heavy load, he made his way over the cobblestone path his father had poured because his mother had always loved them, past the riot of red and yellow tulips blooming in the flower beds, and up to the front door of the house. He knocked, not sure if he should wait or just walk in.

"Just a minute!" a feminine voice called from within. Adam heard bustling behind the door, and Patty, the family's long-time housekeeper, greeted him. Her eyes lit up with delight as she swung the door wide open and pulled him inside. "Adam! I thought it was the postman. Why are you knocking? Get in here." Patty embraced him, and he was engulfed in the scent of chocolate and sugar, overwhelmed by her affection. She pulled back to hold him at arms' length and looked him up and down. She let out a low whistle and said, "You get more handsome every time I see you."

"And you haven't aged a day, Patty. It's so great to see you again." He let her close the door behind him but kept his bags in his hands. "Which room can I take this time?"

"I put fresh sheets and towels in the guest bedroom. You should have everything you need, but let me know if I can pick anything up for you." She followed him across the craftsman style home's living room to the hallway. "Can I get you something from the kitchen?"

"I'm fine for now. I'll take care of myself while I'm here, so don't feel like you need to worry about me." Patty worked for his father, and he wasn't about to take advantage of the sweet woman during his visit, though he knew she would likely dote on him and try to coddle him at every opportunity. After living alone for so long, the relentless attention could be jarring when he first arrived, but he found himself enjoying it once he settled in.

He dropped his bags on the king-size bed that dominated the guest room. Not much had changed since his last visit. The Whitmans were a decidedly masculine group, farmers who worked with their hands. But even without the benefit of his mother's feminine influence, Richard Whitman enjoyed creature comforts. Patty was a tireless worker, even though she was close to retirement age, so the house was always spotless. She'd been with the family as long as Adam could remember, though when he was a kid, the Whitmans were only one of many families she cleaned for. When his mother became ill, she'd moved in and increased her hours, dropping all her other clients. After his wife's death, Adam's father found that he needed Patty more than he thought, and had asked her to stay on until he got back on his feet. Their temporary arrangement had stretched out over five years, and they showed no signs of changing anything. She wasn't much younger than his dad, and it had to be getting close to time for her to retire as well. How would he manage without her?

"I'm making tea, dear, would you like some?" Patty appeared in the doorway and interrupted his thoughts.

He turned to her and nodded. "Sure, that sounds great. I'll join you in a minute." Satisfied, she turned and left him alone again. Patty was never happier than when she was busy caring for others.

He made his way into the kitchen where she'd set out cups for each of them and a plate of cookies, undoubtedly freshly baked. He pulled out a chair and sat beside her. Patty poured him a cup of tea and passed it to him. He murmured his thanks as he blew over the top and inhaled the familiar aroma. If his childhood had a fragrance, it would be of tea. He could close his eyes and recall the aroma of fresh leaves, those drying on the massive trays in the warm, peaceful drying rooms, and the freshly brewed pots of it his family always had at the ready.

"It's great to see you again, sweetheart. We really miss you around here." Patty sipped her own tea and pushed the plate of oversize oatmeal raisin cookies closer to him. Her long, brown hair was pulled back into a low bun, giving her a serious look, but her sweet and generous personality always shined through. No lines marked her face; her skin was as smooth as that of a much younger woman.

He picked a cookie off the plate and took a small bite, enjoying the familiar warm cinnamon flavor. "It's good to be here. I'm definitely due for a break, though if I remember correctly, life on a farm is anything but a vacation." He laughed and sat back in his chair. "Chad and Daniel will never let me get away with resting while I'm here." He could just see them coming by and demanding that he get off his lazy butt and get to work over at the family's resort or restaurant. Operations at the farm were covered, but Adam wouldn't be surprised if he were called upon to get his hands dirty outside, either.

"They'll certainly be happy to see you, but I'm pretty sure Chad and Daniel have everything under control," said Patty gently.

"I'm sure you're right." He drained his cup. "So, do you know where Dad is? Is he planning to come home or should I head over to his office?"

"Richard will be home in a bit; he was planning to be here before you arrived, so he's probably just running a little behind. I think he wants to take you to the office to show you around and get your opinion on some things." Patty rose from her chair and busied herself with clearing the table. He took his cup to the sink and rinsed it out while she filled a rough-hewn hickory bowl with fruits likely pulled straight from the family's gardens.

"Thank you for the tea and cookies. I'm going out for some fresh air." She nodded, humming to herself as she cleaned, and he left through the front door.

He stepped out onto the wraparound porch and was struck by the quiet of his father's suburban neighborhood. Back at home, his life was filled with noise. Chatter, movement, and crowds. At work, everyone bustled around between meetings, running from office to conference room, calling, emailing, and chatting, always chatting. Even at home, people were always coming and going. The silence on his dad's street was deafening, and Adam's hand twitched before automatically reaching for his phone to check email. The sound of a car engine grew louder as it approached, cutting through the quiet. Adam watched the driveway. His father pulled up in a small, black pickup truck, the windows rolled down, his elbow hanging over the driver's side door, and classic country music rolling out of the cab.

"Sorry to keep you waiting. I thought I would beat you home," he called out in greeting. His smile was wide, his excitement at seeing Adam evident. He parked and slid out of the truck, hurrying to meet his son.

The older man, the spitting image of Adam's late grandfather, pulled him into a hug, slapping him on the back a couple of times. "Hi, Dad."

"How was your flight? How have you been?"

"Great. Things are good, really busy, but good. It's nice to get away, though. I didn't realize I needed a break until I got out of the city. Patty's already trying to take care of me, and her cookies are good enough that I might let her. I'm not sure six days here will be enough." He had missed his father more than he realized; it was so good to stand beside him, to see him.

"Things are pretty much the same since last time you were out here, but I wanted to take you out to the farm because I don't know how much you've seen since we expanded. Let me just head in and let Patty know." He squeezed Adam's arm and bounded up to the front door, his speed and enthusiasm that of a younger man.

He came back out with a cookie in hand and a grin on his face.

• • •

Rows of tea plants spread out as far as they could see as they drove past the fields and toward the offices. Beyond the tea, there was a small pear orchard, and to his left were buildings that held processing equipment. Just past the buildings beyond his vision were even more gardens where the family grew produce for their own use and to supply their restaurant and resort. The two pulled into the driveway and hopped out of the truck. Adam was immediately struck by how quiet it was, even though the farm was operating at full speed. It was amazing how a hundred workers could be outside attending to the very busy work of farming without making more noise than a buzz of conversation and the slightest rustling on the breeze as they moved around. Tea leaves were too delicate to be harvested by machine, so everything was done by hand on the farm.

His dad led him away from the small parking lot, his stride brisk. Running such a huge enterprise was an exhausting job; it was no wonder he was ready to hang up his hat. Farming was hard, back-breaking work, a young man's game. Richard Whitman had earned his rest.

They walked down the path to the first building that housed the marketing department office space and storage area. His father opened the door, and a light whoosh of sweet air greeted them. "We've got some new blends, new packaging, things like that. Come on in." He entered a surprisingly modern space, and his shock at the changes must have registered on his face. "Ashley has been hard at work over here. She has a lot of ideas about the brand and thinks that since this place is where most of our local buyers come, it should reflect Emerald Tea Farm in a more sophisticated way. If it were left to me, we'd still have the same old wire shelves and plain paper bags." Dad trailed off as he looked around the space.

Adam took in the gleaming, spotless hardwood floors, the inviting shelves full of neatly organized, beautifully packaged tea products, local artists' work hanging on the walls. His first cousin was right. The old supply building had been barebones and purely utilitarian. The new space was a brilliant showcase for the family products, one that encouraged a leisurely visit. Everything from the soft music playing to the subtle but tempting aroma of the teas begged people to come in. Ashley had even taken the new design a step further, adding a sample bar. He could picture buyers coming in to stock their shops and lingering as they browsed, probably picking up more than they came for. Hell, he knew everything about the tea his family produced but still found himself interested in trying the new blends when they were presented in such a pleasing way. Ashley was a goofy kid growing up, but she had obviously grown into a capable woman. Once again, Richard Whitman demonstrated that he knew how to nurture individual talent by finding the best place for her to shine in the family business.

"The place looks great. Have you seen an increase in sales?" Adam asked.

"We have. Giving Ashley free rein over this place was one of the best decisions I've made lately." He put his hands in his pockets and wandered around, looking at the tea sitting on shelves as Adam admired the changes. A staff member walked in from the storage room in back, balancing boxes in front of her. She greeted the two of them, then set to work restocking shelves and checking inventory.

A soft chime sounded, and they turned to the front door. Adam's heart leapt to his throat when he recognized the woman walking in. "Zoe Miller," he murmured.

Zoe gave his dad a bright smile as she breezed in, bringing sunshine and sweetness with her. That smile fell immediately when her gaze moved to Adam. She quickly recovered and offered him a friendly smile as she approached the pair. Dad enveloped her in a full hug, squeezing a little for extra measure before releasing her. Then Zoe turned to Adam, her clear blue eyes captivating him even as she projected a studied nonchalance.

"Adam, hi," she said as she offered her hand to shake. He took it, struck immediately by how soft and cool her skin was against his. "How have you been?" she asked, sounding polite, as though seeing him was nothing more than a pleasant surprise.

He swallowed, disturbed by how her casual touch could unnerve him, and answered. "I'm great. What are you doing here?" His surprise at seeing her walk through the door and back into his life after avoiding her for the past five years superseded his ability to behave politely.

She laughed, short and without amusement. "I'm just picking up some extra inventory, like I do all the time. What are *you* doing here?" she challenged him, her rosebud lips set in a firm line as she looked up at him. Adam had always towered over her, but she somehow managed to make him feel like he was three feet tall.

"I'm just visiting." His heart was racing in his chest; how could she possibly still have this effect on him after all these years? "Extra inventory for what?"

Zoe gave him a satisfied smile. "I sell and serve your family's tea in my bakery. Business has been good lately." She wandered over to the shelves and surveyed the variety before turning to his dad and asking, "Is there anything new you'd like me to feature?" She ran her fingertips lightly over the bags lined on the shelf.

"We'll probably get something within the next couple of weeks, but there's nothing new since last time you ordered," his dad replied. "The Imperial Jade Chai doesn't sell as well this time of year, so maybe you could push that a bit. I'd hate to end up with a lot of excess inventory."

"You could always send the older teas that don't sell before their expiration date over to the resort. I don't know if Daniel has them on the service menu, but green tea baths and treatments are really popular at spas." She seemed to have forgotten about Adam. She was animated as she considered the possibilities with Dad, beautiful in her enthusiasm. "I'll pair it with some cakes at the shop though. That should help sell it before everybody starts wanting the spring blends."

He watched as she took a few bags of the tea and signed for the order that the employee brought from the back. Funny how he had always successfully avoided running into Zoe when he visited Emerald Springs, until now. Whether he wanted to avoid confrontation or seeing how his desertion had affected her, he wasn't sure. He left for UCLA fifteen years ago after high school graduation, promising they would stay together while he finished his degree. At the time, he meant every word he said, had fully intended to get a degree and go back home to start a life with her. They stayed together long distance for years before he let himself get caught up in southern California's opportunities. He'd landed his dream job and simply couldn't leave it behind, especially since

Zoe's culinary training would have allowed her to work anywhere. She'd planned to join him in California, but their plans fell apart along with her parents' marriage. As far as Adam was concerned, her father's drinking had not only caused the divorce but also his severe depression, which in turn, had Zoe so worried about him that she couldn't leave Emerald Springs. She said she would never forgive herself if something happened to her dad while she was away; even then Zoe was more selfless and mature than Adam, though he didn't see it that way at the time. So he let his new life captivate him and convinced himself he was fine without her. What was he thinking?

As an adult, Zoe had clearly risen above her circumstances and made something of herself. She was positively radiant, and his regret over not trying to keep things together when they briefly reunited after his mother's death now twisted his gut. He'd often thought that ending things the second time was somehow worse than the first, that she knew she'd be foolish to give him a second chance and he'd proved her right. Her face was animated as she chatted about tea and bakeries, her blue eyes flashing with amusement at his father's jokes. He knew he was staring, but he couldn't help it. She was perfect, from her smooth, shapely legs showcased under the red, flared, short skirt of her dress to the cascade of shiny, dark chocolate brown hair falling in waves around her slim shoulders. Everything in between was breathtaking. He thrust his hands in his pockets, feeling awkward and not completely confident he could avoid reaching out to touch her if she got close to him again. Being so close made his fingertips tingle with anticipation. This was ridiculous; he was an adult and they hadn't been together in a long time. He should be able to stand next to her without having a physical reaction.

"Adam, take Zoe's order out to her car, would you?" his dad interrupted his thoughts.

"Sure, no problem." He snapped to attention and headed to the desk. He hoisted the boxes in his arms and followed her out, glad to have something to occupy his hands. She held the door open for him, and he was careful not to brush against her.

They stepped out into the bright sunshine, and she rushed ahead, leaving a light breeze carrying her sweet scent in her wake. Vanilla and sugar, maybe frosting? Whatever it was, she smelled good enough to eat. He followed her to her powder blue Toyota Prius and wished he knew what he should do. His heart wanted to reach out to her, to reconnect, to make amends. His brain knew he would be back in L.A. soon and he should leave her alone. It wouldn't be fair to lead her on, to start something that would only end. Again.

She opened the trunk and he set the boxes inside. He pushed the trunk closed and turned to her, not sure what to say, but sure he didn't want to let her leave. What he wanted to do was pull her close and see if they still fit together, if there was still magic between them. The memory of how soft her hair felt in his hands hadn't faded with the years and miles between them, and he longed to reach out and touch her. Instead, he kept his head down, watching his feet and avoiding eye contact.

"So, thanks for carrying my order out for me. It was nice to see you again." She had her hand on the door handle, and he knew that he likely wouldn't see her again if he didn't say something.

"It was nice to see you, too. Kind of weird, right?" He didn't know what was wrong with him, but his brain appeared to have lost its ability to form intelligent thoughts. The smooth, sophisticated charmer must have fled when faced with the beauty of his first love.

She looked up at him, squinting into the sun, and paused for a beat, as though considering what to say next. "Sure, I guess it is weird seeing you after all this time. I was going to say I'm surprised it hasn't happened before, but I guess I'm not. Not really. It's not really surprising that the same guy who didn't even bother to break up with me properly would avoid me during his visits home. The only real surprise is that it happened at all." She pulled her car door open. He hated being reminded that he had ended their relationship after foolishly rekindling things after his mother's death. Zoe had trusted him not to hurt her, and he had been too afraid to end it like a man, choosing instead to slink back to L.A., leaving behind both Zoe and any chance he had at a real relationship. Perhaps he knew even then that he would stay in Emerald Springs if he allowed himself to return to see her. Back then, nothing had seemed worse than getting stuck in this town.

"Hey, wait. You're right, absolutely right, about everything. I don't know what I was thinking. I know I hurt you, and I shouldn't act like nothing happened. You have every reason to be angry." He tried his most charming smile on her. Surely she felt some of the old spark between them, too. His heart sank when she didn't return the smile, didn't seem affected in the least by him.

"I'm not angry, Adam. I don't stay awake at night wondering why you stopped loving me, or thinking about how much you hurt me when you walked away again. I don't think about you at all." Her voice dropped off at the last word, chilling him.

He cringed and moved back a bit, surprised by her cool dismissal. He put his hands up in front of him, surrendering. "Ouch. I guess I deserved that, but still, ouch."

"I don't mean to hurt you, and I apologize if that sounded harsh. If you'll excuse me, I need to get back to the bakery before my assistant burns the place down. It was nice to see you; I'm sure your dad is glad to have you back home." She smoothed the front of her skirt and straightened her back. He could practically see the wall she erected between them.

"Maybe we can get together before I go back to L.A. I'd like to take you out to dinner or something." He was grasping at straws, but she was about to drive right back out of his life.

"Maybe," she said. "Don't hold your breath, though. I learned my lesson after the last time." She slid into her car and closed the door behind her. He stepped back, not entirely sure she wouldn't run over his foot in her rush to get away from him. He watched her navigate out of the drive and felt his heart drop as she drove out of sight.

Chapter Three

Zoe pulled up in front of Everything Nice and parked, sure she wouldn't be able to propel herself out of the car and into her bakery. With any luck, Adam had believed her when she said she never thought of him. Maybe he'd keep his distance, and she could get on with the business of forgetting him again. Why had he shown up today? Why hadn't Richard warned her he was in town? It had taken months before she could spend time with the Whitmans without thinking of Adam and all that she had lost. In the early days after he broke up with her, while it was still sinking in that he really wasn't coming back home, she retreated into herself. They invited her for dinner every week, like everything was normal, and she declined, sure that they'd lose interest in her just like Adam had. The Whitmans hadn't, though. They'd continued to call and visit until she let them take her into the fold.

Determined not to undo the years of work she had put in to getting over Adam, Zoe pulled herself together and got out of her car. The aroma of fresh cakes and pastries baking wafted through the air, and she was instantly relaxed. No matter what happened in her life, she knew she could find comfort in the kitchen. There, she was in control.

She loaded up her arms with the boxes from Emerald Tea Farm and walked to the door, her head held high. Adam Whitman wouldn't shake her, nor would he so much as distract her today. Her assistant, Courtney, scurried around the counter and made it to the door just in time to hold it open for her. She walked in and let the bakery's familiar warmth envelope her.

"Courtney, could you take these to the back?" She handed the boxes over and shrugged the tote bag holding the tea off her shoulder. After stocking her feature shelf with the boxes, she grabbed a piece of hot pink chalk and scribbled Today's Special: Imperial Jade Chai on her blackboard. They would brew that tea for customers who stayed in the shop and sell the rest for people to take home.

With her task completed, she made her way behind the counter to check on the items in the display case. She straightened the cookies and bars, telling herself she'd forget about Adam before he even left town again, that seeing him hadn't brought everything rushing back. Sure, she had moved on; did she have a choice? Five years was too long to mope around with a broken heart. She'd even let herself fall for another guy, though that had ended even worse than her relationship with Adam. Moving on didn't mean her heart didn't sing at the sight of him; it didn't mean that her fingers didn't itch to reach out and stroke his hair. It only meant she was finally able to make it through her day without yearning for him, without dreaming of him. It meant she could operate her business, maintain her friendships, and hold her head high. It meant she could hear their song without bursting into tears; she could live in Emerald Springs without seeing him everywhere she looked.

She was living her dream, operating a business she built from the ground up, doing what she loved, and doing it well. She was well known and well respected in town, and she had built her reputation on her own, with no help from anyone else. The bell hanging from the door tinkled, and Zoe looked up from the row of orange cranberry oatmeal cookies she was arranging in the case. She straightened, blew her bangs off her forehead, and froze in place when she saw him. Ice water flowed through her veins as her stomach turned over and her throat closed.

Attempting a casual attitude, she forced out, "Hi, Adam."

He walked in, six feet and two inches of heartbreakingly beautiful man, and looked around, taking in the space. Since they parted at the farm, he had obviously regained his composure; too bad she couldn't say the same for herself. He looked relaxed, more like the Whitman that he was, like a guy who could buy half the town if he wanted. The guy who could crook his finger and have any girl come running. He was gorgeous, reminding her so much of the boy she had fallen in love with as a teenager that suddenly she was sixteen and tongue-tied again.

"So, this is your place? It's great." He gave her his signature smile, disarming and sweet.

"Thanks. I'm pretty proud of it." What he was doing, coming to her? She'd been pretty clear she wasn't interested in revisiting their past. Why couldn't he stay away from her so she could start forgetting him again? "What are you doing here?" No need to dance around it; surely they were past playing games.

If he was surprised by her abrupt question, it didn't show. He approached the counter, close enough for her to lean over and touch him. "I came to see you." His deep voice was ripe with possibilities, and she swallowed against the lump forming in her throat. Damn, he was smooth. She saw Courtney grin, clearly eavesdropping, and then quickly pretend to busy herself with cleaning tables. "You left in such a hurry earlier; I didn't get a chance to ask you out. I thought we could grab drinks or something after you close tonight."

She was speechless for a moment. Fifteen years ago, he slid a promise ring on her finger, vowing to replace it with an engagement ring after he graduated from UCLA. But years of long-distance dating, endless phone calls and constant emails, and visits back and forth hadn't been enough to keep them together. Seven years ago, he decided their relationship was over if she wasn't willing to move to Los Angeles. It tore her apart to let him go, but she needed more time at home to make sure her dad would be okay after the divorce. Adam didn't want to hear it; he was so cold, he forced her to choose. In that moment, Adam Whitman threw away everything they meant to each other.

Now he thought drinks were appropriate?

"Why?" she asked, knowing it sounded blunt and probably rude, but she didn't care.

She wasn't ready to move backward, and by the looks of him, it wouldn't take much to send her on that path. Been there, done that. Then five years ago, she'd let herself believe they had a chance, only to watch him walk away from her—from them—again.

He put his hands up and dipped his head, looking irresistible. It was maddening, really. "I guess I deserve that. Tomorrow is family dinner night, and I know you usually go. When I'm not in town, at least. If you don't want to skip it this week, I thought it would be a little less awkward if we caught up together beforehand. I could swing by after you close tonight, and we could walk over to Coffee Queen for a little dinner or just go for drinks at The Rusty Tap if you want. What do you think? You wouldn't be trapped in a car with me or anything." He looked both hopeful and confident.

She did eat dinner with the Whitmans every week, without fail, and she didn't want to skip it just because Adam finally blew into town. They were the closest thing she had to a family since her parents divorced. Her mom split town and her father finally gave up trying to stay sober, leaving her rudderless without their drama consuming her life. The Whitmans' dinner was something she looked forward to, and she'd earned her spot at the table.

Adam did have a point; things would be a lot more comfortable if they had already put aside any awkwardness between them. Besides, what could a quick meal or a few beers together hurt? She should be able to handle a conversation with the man. She was a successful, confident woman who didn't live in the past, right? Perhaps if she repeated it often enough, it could become true. "All right, I'll have drinks with you. I can leave here at five."

His face lit up, giving her heart a little hitch. "Great, see you at five." He tapped out a little rhythm on the display case before turning and leaving the bakery. She couldn't help but watch as he left. The view was just as nice coming as going.

Hey, they weren't getting back together, so what was the harm in looking?

Courtney left the towel on the table she had polished until the finish practically wore off and hurried over to Zoe, a mischievous grin on her face. "Oh my gosh, who was that tall piece of man candy?"

She raised an eyebrow. "Man candy? That was Adam Whitman."

"Like the tea farm, restaurant, and resort Whitmans?" Courtney's eyes were wide. Zoe sometimes forgot the Whitmans were a big deal in Emerald Springs. They were as much a part of her as anyone could be; it was easy to lose sight of how the rest of the town saw them.

"The very same."

"And he had to practically beg you just to have drinks with him? He'd have to beg me to stay away from him. What is wrong with you, woman?" Courtney didn't try to hide her amazement.

"Adam and I used to go out. We've been broken up for a long time, and I don't see much point in spending time together when he's going back home soon. He lives in Los Angeles, so there's really no reason for us to get cozy again just because he's here for a visit." It had to be a good sign that she was so mentally healthy, she could talk about the man who broke her heart without her voice so much as wavering. Although, saying they used to go out was the understatement of the year.

Courtney raised one eyebrow, skeptical. "Well, if you say so. I'm pretty sure most girls would be glad to have any excuse to cozy up with him. You must have some kind of iron willpower."

"Something like that," she said. *More like a strong sense of self-preservation.* She glanced up at the clock. "Can you hold down the fort up here? I've got some paperwork to do."

Courtney agreed and busied herself with straightening up the counter. Paperwork and bookkeeping were always piling up on her desk. Crunching some numbers would get her mind off Adam. Maybe. It was worth a try.

• • •

Adam walked down Spruce Street, past Bev's Used Books and Valley Pharmacy, but his mind was on Zoe rather than familiar sights. Seeing her again after so much time had hit him harder than he would have imagined. Family dinner would be awkward if she decided to fling more verbal barbs his way, but it was the price of doing business. He knew he had hurt her, unforgivably, and he deserved her wrath. He'd pushed the guilt aside for so many years, it was even more painful when it came rushing back. And it wouldn't stay away now that he'd seen her, seen all that he'd given up for the second time five years ago. That was one of the big regrets of his life. They could move on from the relationship, but he would always regret ending things so abruptly. He'd taken the coward's way out, offering nothing more than a phone call as he went back to L.A. The fact that she was willing to meet with him meant either she really did care nothing for him, or perhaps she felt the same spark he did. His policy of never staying in Emerald Springs for more than a few days was a sensible one; when he was in and out of town in the space of a weekend, he could leave it behind. He was getting in too deep already. Between reconnecting with Zoe and the beauty of Emerald Springs, L.A. was starting to look dull and lifeless in comparison.

He checked his watch and looked around the shops crowding the town's charming downtown area for somewhere to kill time until Zoe closed her bakery. A man with a scruffy beard, unkempt hair, and loose, wrinkled clothes caught Adam's attention; everyone else out on the street blended into the picture-perfect small town scene. Even more unusual, the man looked oddly familiar. As he approached, Adam wracked his brain trying to place him.

"Hey, Adam! Long time no see, huh?" The hearty greeting stirred something, something like disgust. He knew this man from the past, but his identity was eluding him.

"Hey," he said. At work, he encountered situations like this all the time and it was rare that he had such a visceral reaction when trying to figure out how he knew someone.

The man laughed, hoarse and scratchy. "It's me, Marlon. Marlon Miller? It's been a while."

"Of course, hey Marlon. How are you? It has been a while." Adam recovered from his surprise at meeting Zoe's father on the street and attempted to make normal conversation.

Marlon clapped him on the shoulder. "I can't complain, man. It's all good." He could smell alcohol on the guy's breath and carefully kept his expression neutral.

"So, you still live in town?" It was the first question he could come up with.

"Nah, man, my old lady split, and I lost the house. I live out in Meyerville, got a little place. I'm working as a handyman at Split Acres now. It's only part-time, but I need the money." Marlon looked like he might have indulged in more than just alcohol, and it was only four-thirty in the afternoon.

"Split Acres, huh? How do you like it over there?" From what he had heard, Joe Sanders was in a bit of financial trouble, and the Whitmans were hoping to buy some of his land. Joe was still bitter over the split and apparently would rather run the farm into the ground than sell to Richard Whitman, so the proposal might be a tough sell.

"I can't complain. Like I said, I need the money. It was a pretty sweet gig for a while, but Colleen started butting into her dad's business and had me bumped down to part-time," Marlon grumbled and pushed his hands in his pockets. Adam had grown up with Colleen Sanders, had in fact spent as much time with her as with his own brothers when their fathers were partners. From what he heard from his family, she had grown up to be a competent businesswoman who handled the challenges her father apparently couldn't. Obviously, she was a sore spot with Marlon, though as far as Adam could tell, Colleen was the only reason Split Acres didn't belong to the bank. She spent the time she could be using to expand the farm's operations putting out fires and keeping the whole thing afloat.

"Well, Marlon, it was nice to see you. Maybe we'll run into each other again before I go home." He held out his hand, and the man shook it.

"All right, buddy. See you around." Marlon hesitated instead of walking away, his expression blank.

"All right then," said Adam.

He ducked into Emerald Springs Florist, grateful to get away and end that strange encounter. Marlon Miller had never been father of the year material, spending Zoe's childhood and teen years falling deeper into drinking and depression, and moving farther away from the things productive citizens did. Like remaining sober during working hours or being able to stop drinking when it was tearing his marriage apart. He never would've guessed he'd fallen so far though, and finally saw why Zoe was so concerned that she couldn't leave Emerald Springs once her mother left town and Marlon was on his own. At the time, he'd thought Marlon was a worthless drunk whose drinking had caused both his divorce and the severe depression that had Zoe so worried. Whether that was true or not, Zoe was probably smart to realize that her father needed her.

"Is that Adam Whitman I see in my shop?" A slim brunette in her early fifties emerged from the back, wiping her hands on a pink apron and smiling widely.

"Hi, Mrs. Moore." He met her halfway across the shop by a cooler containing buckets of roses and accepted her hug.

"It's Kathleen. Mrs. Moore sounds like an old lady. What are you doing in town?" She clicked her tongue as she reluctantly released her hold on him, clearly pleased to see him.

"I'm visiting the farm to help my dad out. I'll just be here about a week before I have to get back to L.A."

"Well, goodness, it sure is nice to see you. Have you seen Zoe Miller? She has her own bakery right down the street." He figured nobody in this town would ever think of either of them without the other. "Yes, as a matter of fact, I'm going to take her out for drinks tonight so we can catch up."

Kathleen's eyes gleamed mischievously. "Just drinks, huh?" She nudged him and winked.

He laughed. "Yes, just drinks." It wouldn't be enough for him, but he knew better than to push his luck. Zoe could reconstruct the wall between them at the slightest provocation.

"Well, of course you'll want to take her some flowers. Let's see what we've got." Kathleen's tone told him that saying no wasn't an option.

She flitted over to the refrigerated case, opened the door, and waited for him to join her. "The tulips are really nice this time of year. We could put together a beautiful arrangement; what do you think?"

Without waiting for an answer, Kathleen began plucking tulips from their containers. He hadn't planned on buying flowers for Zoe, but since he was here, he had to admit it was a great idea. It was a perfect offering for someone trying to assuage his own guilt; he just hoped Zoe wouldn't see it that way. Kathleen gathered tulips in pink, red, and white as she hummed to herself. She undoubtedly thought she was taking part in his romantic plans and had dreams of providing their wedding flowers dancing around in her head. Zoe clearly had no interest in romance with him, but surely she would appreciate a beautiful arrangement of flowers. Kathleen left to arrange the tulips and he wandered around the store, his hands in his pockets. Much of his life had been accented by flowers from this shop. He bought Zoe's homecoming and prom corsages here, not to mention several orders he'd called in to have delivered to her during their long-distance relationship. His mother's funeral flowers came almost exclusively from the shop; Kathleen was the only florist in town, and everybody sent arrangements to pay their respects.

Kathleen returned carrying a pink-tinted glass vase bursting with the tulips. They were certainly romantic, but Zoe's chilly reception told him it would take more than flowers from the local florist for her to warm up to him. It was a start, though, and he could use all the help he could get. He approached the counter and pulled his wallet from his pocket.

"Don't worry about it, hon. Just call me cupid." Kathleen waved away his credit card.

"Nonsense, Kathleen. This is at least a fifty dollar arrangement; I insist on paying." He handed her his card.

"Fifty dollars? You've been in the big city too long. It's thirty dollars, young man." She accepted his card and slid it through her card reader. "Thank you."

"No, thank you, ma'am. This is beautiful and I'm sure Zoe will love it." He took the flowers and let Kathleen get past him to walk him to the entrance. She opened the door for him, looking pleased, and he promised to stop in again soon as he stepped out into the late afternoon sunshine. He walked down to Everything Nice to pick up Zoe for their date that wasn't really a date and was surprised to see the door propped open. He stepped in to the shop and wrinkled his nose as the acrid smell of smoke hit him. That explained it.

"Zoe?" he called out, waving his hand in front of his face and squinting his eyes against the burning smoke.

Her employee stepped around the counter to greet him. "She's in the back; just a second."

Zoe came through a door, her hair in a disheveled ponytail, her apron covered in flour. "Hey," she said. She ran the back of her hand across her forehead and gave him a sheepish look. "I lost track of time and burned a loaf of bread."

"So that explains the smell. Are you okay?" She seemed much more frazzled than he would expect. Surely this wasn't the first time she had burned something.

"Yeah, I'm fine, just a little rattled. My dad stopped in, and I'll just say it didn't end well. I'll be fine; I always am." She was a survivor, a fighter, but she looked so fragile when she was sad. If he hadn't been holding the vase of flowers, he'd be tempted to scoop her into his arms and hold her.

"Did something happen between you two?"

"Nothing crazy, just more of the same. He got it in his head that I have a lot of money to spare, even went so far as to make a lame 'rolling in the dough' joke." She smiled sadly. "He just wants money. That's what it always boils down to; he needs money, he thinks I have it, and he thinks I owe him."

"I'm sure that's hard for you, especially after all you've done for him. I doubt he realizes how much you've given up for him." He shifted his weight, eager to lighten the mood, and handed her the tulips . "These are for you."

"They're gorgeous. Thank you." He could swear tears were brimming in her eyes, and the vulnerability stirred something in him. He wanted to read more into it, to think that his return was affecting her, but she was probably just emotionally fragile from the encounter with her father. Any act of kindness could soften her right now; it had little to do with him. She turned away and set the vase on the white marble counter by the cash register. "You didn't have to do that."

He kept the tone light. "I stopped in Kathleen's shop and told her we were going out for drinks, so yeah, I had to do it. I clearly had no choice."

He looked around the bakery, impressed by her simple but sophisticated style. Zoe's signature was on every aspect of the shop. The shabby chic white shelves were immaculate and held beautifully arranged products for sale, many of which were from Emerald Tea Farm. The bakery case was full of decadent-looking confections: cupcakes, cookies, muffins, each pastry more mouthwatering than the last.

He indicated the bakery case and changed the subject, ready for the sadness lingering in her eyes to disappear. "What do you do with all the things you don't sell at the end of the day?"

She looked animated for the first time since he'd crossed paths with her today, and he was glad to get her mind off of her father and how closely his condition was tied into the end of their relationship. "Ashley comes by in the morning and packs everything up for the Emerald Springs Senior Day Center. They serve it for breakfast along with tea your dad sends. None of it is so old that it's not good. It's just not cool to sell day-old pastries when I promise everything is freshly baked."

"I had no idea you two were working together." He was more than a little pleased that his cousin and family business were involved with Zoe's charitable activities, and it was good to see her find an organization where her compassion for senior citizens was appreciated. It was just further proof that Zoe was as much a Whitman as he was, probably more so.

"It's a small thing, really. I certainly ate enough free breakfasts as a kid. The least I can do is send over a few muffins and give back a little." He could remember her sitting in the grade school cafeteria every morning, wearing someone else's cast off clothes, chowing down on muffins and milk. Zoe had gone from that scrawny kid to a beautiful firecracker of a teenager.

"It's not a small thing, babe." The endearment slipped out before he could stop himself, and she flinched almost imperceptibly. "I'm impressed, really impressed. I'm sure they're grateful to have your help, and the seniors are getting the best breakfast in town."

She looked pleased. "It's nothing. I can even write it all off every year. Let's get out of here before I get a big head." She smiled at him, and he knew he was smiling back like an idiot, but he couldn't help himself. The magic of her opening up to him, even a little, was encouraging.

"I'll come down early in the morning and finish cleaning everything up." She untied her apron and flung it carelessly on the counter.

"Come down?"

"I live in the apartment upstairs." She gestured to the ceiling.

"That's very convenient."

"Oh yeah, especially considering how early I get up. Let's roll, before I change my mind and go upstairs to crawl in bed instead." She pulled the strap of her purse over her shoulder. "Courtney, would you mind locking up after you're finished? I'll handle everything we didn't get to when I come in tomorrow morning."

"Sure thing." Courtney picked up her supplies and left the beverage station that she had been cleaning while she pretended not to listen to their conversation.

"Shall we, then?" He led Zoe to the door with his hand at the small of her back, loving the way they fit together in even the smallest way. It would be far wiser to keep his distance, to not lead her on, but he found it nearly impossible to stay away. She stepped out onto the sidewalk, out of his reach, and pulled the elastic out of her ponytail, shaking her hair loose and bringing the subtle scent of her shampoo into his space. He turned away as she pulled a tube of shimmery lip gloss from her handbag. His willpower was fading fast; he couldn't watch her swipe the gloss across her lips and expect to keep his hands to himself. He let her walk a few steps in front of him as they made their way down the street to the bar, sure that he would take her hand in his if they were close enough.

...

They walked into The Rusty Tap side by side but not touching, and were enveloped in the bar's low hum of conversation. Zoe let her eyes adjust and shot a quick glance toward the stools lining the bars to see if her father was among the early evening crowd. Adam looked like he might offer his arm as he led her inside, but she kept enough distance to discourage him. She hated to admit it, but if he offered, she knew she'd take it. Her attraction to him was disappointing; as far as she was concerned, she was well over him and intended to keep it that way. Why then was she struggling to keep her hands off of him? Surely five years was long enough to kill off the last remaining feelings she might have for him. Why hadn't the physical pull she always felt toward him weakened with the years, too?

He turned to her, inclining his head so that his lips were close to her ear. A tiny shiver skittered through her at his warm breath on her skin. "Want to get a booth?"

She swallowed. It was far wiser to sit at a table close to the window, or better yet, at the bar, but she nodded and he led her across the room to a cozy booth in a dim corner of the bar. He placed his hand on the small of her back as they reached the booth, and by sheer force of will, she kept her eyes trained on the table and slipped out of his reach. It would have been so easy, and so foolish, to look up to see if his eyes reflected the same longing she felt. She scooted onto the bench over the cracked red vinyl and watched as he folded himself on the other side. His large frame filled the space across from her, and she was certain she could smell him in their close quarters, a sophisticated scent that was both fresh and exotic, and wholly out of place in the shabby booth. A waitress approached the table, and Zoe let her eyes flit across Adam's face as she turned to greet her. Their eyes met for an awkward second before he turned his attention to the waitress and gave her a charming smile.

"Hi guys, I'm Samantha. What can I get for you?" The waitress addressed both of them, but Zoe noted with irritation that she only had eyes for Adam. Why did she even care if another woman found him attractive? He hadn't been hers for a long time.

He turned to Zoe. "Do you want a cocktail, or should we share a pitcher?" He put his hands on the table, close enough to touch if she reached over.

"Beer would be great." She kept her hands folded in her lap.

"Great, I'll be right back." The waitress gave Adam a flirty smile and headed through crowd to the mirror-backed bar lined with liquor bottles and glassware, her hips swaying much more than necessary.

Adam didn't notice any of the show; his eyes were on Zoe. He'd always been able to make her feel like she was the only girl in the room. She quickly looked down at the table and pushed her hair behind her ear. As nervous as she was, he was cool and comfortable.

He leaned back in the booth and laid an arm across the back of his seat. "I can't believe you've been open for three years and this is the first time I've been in your bakery."

"Well, your dad and brothers certainly come in often enough. I'm surprised, too." This was a subject she could feel comfortable about. She loved her work and enjoyed talking about it.

"You always were a great baker, but I would've pictured you ending up in some fancy restaurant, after going through culinary school."

"I thought about it, but I don't love it enough to put up with the insane working conditions in a restaurant kitchen. Once

I figured that out, I got into the specialty desserts and breads program at SCA, and the rest is history." While Adam was at UCLA, she'd gone to Seattle Culinary Academy, though he'd never shown much interest in her studies. He was so wrapped up in his environmental engineering program, he rarely asked what she was learning in culinary school.

"I would have worried about opening up a bakery so close to the diner, but it was obviously a smart move. Your shop fits in perfectly here since the menus are so different from one another."

"Yeah, I couldn't have found a better location and the other downtown merchants are great to work with. Except for Sam, of course." She covered her mouth with her hand and laughed. "Oops, sorry."

His easy smile relaxed her. "That's okay. I only claim him because he's my uncle. So he gave you trouble?"

His dad's brother had opened the Coffee Queen diner almost four years ago in an attempt to appease his now-ex-wife, who desperately wanted to be married to a successful businessman. Sam's heart was never in the business, and it showed in everything from his poor management to his willingness to sell to the first available buyer when times got tough. "I can laugh about it now, but he was so hard on me, and it was such a surprise, you know? I guess he's less like your dad than I thought."

"They're about as different as night and day."

"Absolutely. Your dad was so supportive and did so much to help me get started, but Sam complained about everything he could. I thought a bakery and a diner could peacefully coexist, that we were different enough we weren't really competitors, but he apparently thought I was out to destroy his business. It was ridiculous."

"I'm sure that was frustrating for you, but it doesn't really surprise me. He's always been more willing to shoot other people down than to worry about his own business."

He looked up as the waitress approached the table. With a smile aimed only at him, she handed each of them a mug and poured two beers before leaving the pitcher on the table. "Can I get you two anything else? The kitchen's open." She laid a hand on her notepad sitting in her apron pocket and pushed a hip out as she waited for their response.

Adam raised his eyebrows at Zoe. "You sure you don't want to get something to eat?"

She shook her head. "I'm good for now, thanks." She offered the waitress a smile that subtly suggested the woman check on her other tables. Then Zoe took the mug in both hands and settled back in the booth. "So what brings you home?"

"My dad's ready to retire and doesn't know how to turn things over, or even who to turn them over to. He used to ask me to take over when it came time, but he hasn't come right out and said he wants that again. I came up so we could talk about it more, maybe figure something out. At this point, I'm hoping he might be ready to hire a manager so he could still ultimately be in charge. I could always be available for consultation if he found someone to manage the day-to-day operations."

"Consultation? Do you think you know enough about the farm to do that?" She took a long pull from her beer and let the cool alcohol warm her from the inside out.

"I did grow up on the farm, if you remember. I know every step in the process, and I've had to do everything at one time or another, you know." He sounded more defensive than someone who didn't want the farm should sound, but she let it slide.

"If you say so," she said with a nod. "I think you might be surprised to find how much the farm has changed since the last time you worked on it."

His dismissing the idea that he might come home to help with the family business reminded Zoe that he wasn't the man for her any more. She'd let some of the old feelings in; whether they were nostalgia or loneliness she didn't know, but it was time to tuck those back deep inside her heart where they belonged. He made his choice, and it wasn't her. It wasn't even his home and family. It was his career and life in Los Angeles. She had only to think back to the first couple years after he left home for UCLA, back when she thought things were going to work out, to remember why she was so bitter now. It was at her high school graduation when Adam came home to celebrate with her that she started to think of his family as hers. Her own parents didn't so much as put in an appearance at the ceremony, but the Whitmans applauded her as they would their sons. Little did she know then that she'd be more involved with the Whitmans than Adam would be as time went on. It was Zoe who sat at the family dinner table like clockwork, Zoe who sat with Richard for hours day after day when Sheila passed away, Zoe who baked cookies for the Whitman men when they needed a little cheer. She had found her place in the family, out of love and necessity, and it had nothing to do with Adam anymore.

They sat in silence, each feeling the awkwardness that unfolded once the farm and its future came up. She watched his eyes wander around the bar, wondering what he was thinking.

He broke the silence first. "So, are you seeing anyone?"

She had to laugh; he didn't beat around the bush. "Not right now, no. Why?"

"I was just wondering." He picked up his beer mug. "I wanted to make sure there wasn't some guy who'd want to kick my ass for taking you out tonight."

"You're safe for now." She took a long sip from her own mug and watched him over the rim. The alcohol was working its magic, and she enjoyed loose feeling spreading through her limbs. She was feeling better already, starting to forget about her father and the fact that the man who'd broken her heart was sitting across from her, casually catching up on her life.

"Phew, thank goodness," he joked. She let her guard down a bit; they weren't the same old Adam and Zoe from the early days, but they could get along while he was in town at least. If the past was any indicator, he'd be gone before these old feelings became new ones. Long before she remembered how it felt to be in his arms, his lips brushing against hers. She stopped herself and sat up straight, clearing her head. The past was a dangerous path to go down.

"What about you?"

"I'm not seeing anyone right now."

"Not right now? But surely there's been someone." She probably didn't want to know, but the alcohol made her bold.

He ran his fingertip over the rim of his glass. "Sure, I've dated since we ... since I left." He cleared his throat. "Mostly women from work, I've been set up a few times, things like that. Nobody special."

"In all this time? Nothing serious?"

"Nothing has worked out. You know, I'm busy, and it's hard to find someone who understands and is willing to accommodate my schedule."

She scoffed. "Well, when you put it that way, I can see why you're still single."

"Hey, come on. It's not easy to strike a balance."

"I'll bet." It was even harder when you thought your job was more important than everyone else's and didn't particularly want to strike a balance, but she kept that to herself. The past was just that, and there was no need to be rude. "I'd think if you dated someone from work, that would be easier, though."

"I thought so, but it wasn't. The few times I tried, they had schedules just as demanding as mine, and sometimes we were competing for the same accounts. After a while, it became easier to just stay single."

"Wow. Being single isn't the end of the world, but I wouldn't choose it just because it's easier." And there was one of their fundamental differences. Zoe cared about family, community, being a part of something bigger than herself. It didn't seem like Adam saw much farther than his own nose these days.

"If I want to get anywhere with my company, I have to stay focused." He shrugged and topped off their drinks. "I've put in too much time and effort to push it aside."

"You really don't think you can have both?"

"I haven't managed that yet. If I'm not working on accounts, I'm scouting them. Then I'm researching the clients as well as the technology and programs that will suit their needs, and after that I'm courting them. Eco Initiatives might as well be my wife." Zoe thought of the bone-deep joy she found in owning her own business, in her relationships, and her ties to the community, and thought that Adam's pseudo-marriage to a job was sad.

As they finished the pitcher, they caught up on the superficial details of each other's lives, moving away from the topics that reminded them too much of their past. Zoe was relieved to find she thought her own life was more interesting than his, that staying in Emerald Springs wasn't a mistake. When Adam was at UCLA, he was so focused on finishing school and landing that first job. Once he got his dream job at Eco Initiatives, he talked of almost nothing else. At first, she wrote it off as his excitement, but after a while she feared that his enthusiasm for the job was all-consuming, that she couldn't compare. Moving to L.A. to be with him would've been the end of everything she'd known, and she couldn't trust his feelings enough to be sure that it was worth it.

Adam settled the bill, and they scooted across the vinyl booths. He again rested his hand on the small of her back, and despite her resolve, she felt that old attraction demanding attention again. She made the mistake of glancing up at him, only to see that he was already looking down at her, a wistful expression on his face.

She'd seen that look before, and it led to nothing but trouble. When Sheila Whitman passed away, they'd been unable to avoid each other when he came to Emerald Springs for the funeral. A look like the one he was wearing tonight made her forget the pain of losing him long enough to fool herself into thinking that it could work between them again. She wouldn't make that mistake a third time.

As they wound their way through the crowd to the exit, more than one woman checked Adam out. There was a time when he was as much a part of her as the air she breathed; it was easy then to forget how handsome he was. Now she needed to focus on getting through his visit without thinking of him as a man, without losing her heart yet again.

Chapter Four

Adam stopped on the sidewalk in front of her bakery and turned to Zoe, who was already pulling her keys out of her handbag. Not sure what he wanted to happen next, but sure he wasn't ready to let her go, he struggled for something else to say. If he knew what was good for him, he'd say goodnight and let her walk into her shop and out of his sight. He'd see her at the family dinner and then get his ass back to L.A. and forget all about her. He wouldn't think about what her hair would feel like in his hands, or if her lips still felt the same opening under his own. He'd forget how their bodies fit together perfectly, how her fingers laced with his.

"Do you want me to walk you up?" he asked. He should get in his car and drive away. He shouldn't try to get back on her good side, and he definitely shouldn't start thinking of her as his. It couldn't possibly end well, so why did he keep edging closer to her? Maybe it was the beautiful night reminding him of their past, or maybe it was the way her hair smelled like vanilla, but Adam was flirting with disaster here. He knew he had to leave, but he wanted to pull her into his arms and kiss her, just once. What if she said yes, though? Then what would he do?

She regarded him with amusement, clearly not as conflicted as he. "I think I can make it fine on my own."

She could see right through him and he was an idiot. That's what happened when you started feeling nostalgic back in your hometown with your high school sweetheart. The feelings weren't real, and he could push them aside on a moment's notice.

He rocked back on his heels and attempted a casual, friendly tone. "All right then. I guess I'll see you tomorrow night."

"Thanks for the drink and the conversation. I definitely needed that tonight, and I think you're right about it making things easier at family dinner. We should be able to make it through a meal together without too much trouble. See you tomorrow, I guess." She turned and disappeared into her building without looking back. He watched her skirt swish around her legs and wished he knew what he wanted. He couldn't commit to her. He couldn't ask her to forget their past and reconnect just for the time he was in town. So he wouldn't allow himself to spend his visit mooning over Zoe. It wasn't fair to her, for one thing. It would be selfish to indulge himself after the way he'd treated her. And he didn't want to give her any false hope or ideas about reuniting when he'd be back in L.A. by the end of next week. It didn't matter how the years had only made Zoe more beautiful, how much he wanted to follow her into her apartment and kiss her senseless.

He realized he was still standing on the sidewalk like a lost puppy and got in his car, hoping she hadn't seen him standing there long after she left. He cranked up the radio, rolled the windows down, and headed back to the house for the night.

•••

He walked up the porch steps and fished his keys out of his pocket, humming to himself. His key slipped in the lock, and Adam wondered who was in the house. His dad's truck wasn't in the driveway, so he assumed he had returned to the office. Easing the door open, he heard his brothers' voices.

"Mystery solved," he said in greeting. Chad and Daniel looked up from their seats on the couches and held beer bottles up in greeting. "I was worried I'd left the door unlocked and the lights on."

"It probably happens to you all the time, at your advanced age," Chad teased.

"I told Dad he might want to disconnect the gas while you were here, just in case," said Daniel.

"Screw you," he retorted. "With age comes wisdom. Besides, I'm sure Patty will make sure I don't burn the place down." That earned him a laugh from his brothers, and he dropped his keys and wallet on the table.

He joined them in the living room, taking a seat next to Chad on the big, brown leather couch in front of the fireplace. Chad pulled a bottle out of a cooler at his side and passed it to Adam. He fished a bottle opener out of the side table drawer and handed it over, too. Adam turned the bottle around in his hand, noting there was no label.

"Thanks. Is this one of yours?"

"Yep. It's a new batch and I wanted you guys to try it." Chad was a talented home brewer and had experimented with growing hops on the Whitman farm. His blends were inventive and bold, and Adam always looked forward to trying Chad's newest concoction.

He popped the top open and took a sip of the icy brew. "Damn, that's good."

"Yeah? I'm calling it Porch Swing. Can you taste the grapefruit and ginger?" Chad was justifiably proud of his brew.

"Yeah, and there's something else. What is that?" Adam took another swig from the bottle and tried to place the flavor. "Is it lime?"

"Yep. You think it works?" Chad sat forward and watched their reactions.

"Definitely. This is really good. One of the best you've come up with lately," Daniel said.

"It's probably my favorite of yours that I've tried," said Adam as he settled into the cushions and took another pull from the bottle. "So did you two just miss me or is something going on?"

"We figured if we wanted to spend any time with you before you head home, we'd have to catch you here. We never know how long you'll stay. You're probably heading back to L.A. soon, right?" Daniel sat back in his chair and picked up his beer.

"I don't know, man. I think I might be sticking around a while this time," said Adam. "I've got a week off work, and from the sound of it, most of it's going to be spent with Dad. He seems to have a lot on his mind." He paused for effect. "And I just got back from seeing Zoe."

Chad choked a little on his drink and pounded his chest a few times. "Come again?"

Daniel laughed. "Zoe Miller? I'm surprised she gave you the time of day."

He gave his brothers a mock wounded look. "Is that so hard to believe? We had a good time."

"I'm sure you did; she's too nice to tell you to go to hell. I always thought she let you off too easy," Chad said.

"Well, she made a point to tell me she never thinks about me before agreeing to go out for drinks," Adam said with a laugh. "That certainly hurt."

"You know you deserved it though," Daniel began. "You weren't here to see what happened after you ended things with her after Mom died. If it's possible, I think she took it harder the second time, and for a while we weren't sure if she was going to be okay. I can't for the life of me understand why you thought you could start up with her again."

"It was months before we could convince her to join us for dinner again. She'd gone every single week up until you broke up with her, then just like that," Chad said with a snap of his fingers, "she didn't want to go, probably didn't want any reminder of your ugly mug. It was a tough time for her. She only started coming to dinner again when Ashley literally drove to her apartment and picked her up. Even then it was a while before she was her old self."

"I've asked myself why I didn't just leave her alone a thousand times. I knew I wasn't going to stay in town, but I guess it didn't matter to me then. That was such a hard time for everyone, you know? Back then, it seemed like we needed each other, though, just to get through it. I didn't realize she took it so hard. Not that I stuck around to find out." Adam laughed without humor and ran his fingers through his hair.

"I doubt she wanted you to feel sorry for her." Daniel sat forward and rested his elbows on his knees. "I'm sure she kept it to herself for a reason."

"Yeah, she didn't want your pity any more than she's ever wanted anybody's. You know her; she'll do anything to avoid people feeling like she needs to be rescued." Chad took a long drink from his bottle.

"I know. I'm glad you guys were here to help her."

"She's family." Daniel shrugged.

"Yeah, we see her way more often than we see you," Chad teased.

Adam winced at the reminder and got up to put his empty bottle in the recycling bin.

• • •

Adam sipped from his travel mug of Cherry Berry Spice tea and waited for his father to arrive, enjoying the quiet morning on the porch of his childhood home. His dad had left early that morning to attend to some unnamed business and was to meet Adam at the farm to spend the day together. He'd fallen into the habit of drinking coffee in L.A. and rarely spent the time to make a cup of tea.

A small part of him acknowledged he might have subconsciously stopped drinking tea so he'd separate more from home, from this life. But Patty had brewed it before he left the house this morning, and he didn't feel he could refuse.

In the distance, he could hear the early morning shift workers, but the front porch was peaceful enough to allow him to get lost in his thoughts. He breathed in the fresh spring air along with the subtle aroma of his tea as he rocked the old wooden chair against the planks. The chair groaned under his weight, and he stretched his legs out in front of him. He couldn't remember the last time a morning had been so unscheduled. His jaw tightened just thinking of the meetings he should be preparing for at work but was missing, the bustle of employees at their cubicles, months of work coming to fruition. At his desk, he'd be surrounded by the sound of ringing phones and chattering workers instead of birds chirping and wind rustling the leaves on trees. He'd be doing something, not sitting around while everyone around him worked. If he took the promotion, things would heat up even more, and he'd have more control over priorities, resource allocation, staffing.

Tires crunched on gravel, and his dad pulled up in the driveway only a few minutes late.

Dad hopped down from his pickup truck, a wide smile on his face as he slammed the door shut behind him. "Good morning. Looks like you're ready to roll." He approached the porch, and Adam stood to greet him. Instead, his dad brought Adam in for a brief hug as he slapped him on the back a few times.

Adam turned halfway to the door. "Do you want to go in and get a drink or something?"

"No, thanks. Patty left me breakfast to go, so I'm fine." Adam was glad to see his father smiling and happy again. He should visit more often.

He finished the last of his tea and set the travel mug on a side table. "Let's get to it, then."

He followed his father down the steps and into a garage near the house. Dad took the driver's seat in a golf cart and patted the vinyl seat beside him. "Ready to roll?"

Adam plopped down and laughed to himself. Things really had changed if they weren't going to tour the farm on foot. "We've got to drive? Just how far are we going today?"

"I thought I'd show you the whole property, really give you a good idea of what we're working with now. Besides, we're strictly organic. You can't go tromping through the fields like you did when you were a kid." He backed out of the space and navigated the cart over the path past the house and toward the plants and processing buildings.

To their right, verdant fields of tea stretched over acres of land as far as Adam could see. The sweet Washington spring air blew across his face and through his hair as they bumped over the path.

His father pointed to the right. "We've tripled in size since the last time you came out here."

"Dad, it's not like I'm never here. You couldn't have grown that much since Christmas." Despite himself, he felt his dad's enthusiasm and pride pull at his heart.

"I mean the last time you really came out here, out to the fields. I don't remember you leaving my house at Christmas." He nudged him with his elbow and grinned. "City boy," he teased.

"All right, you got me there. Damn, that's a lot of tea." He was awed by the sheer size of it. Operations had more than tripled since the last time he'd been out past the house, no exaggeration. How had he spent so many years ignoring the farm? Was he that determined to forget his past, to convince himself he wasn't interested?

"Yep, it sure is." They navigated past fields of plants on the right, and buildings where tea leaves were withered and dried on the left. They came upon gardens, and his dad pointed to rows of vegetables sprouting up nicely. "Everything's looking good this year. I'd like to expand out further," he spread his hand past Adam, "and add more. I don't want to see so much Whitman land covered in grass. Seems like such a waste."

They reached the edge of the path and parked the cart just short of an orchard. His dad hopped off his seat and stretched before heading into the clearing with Adam following. They made their way past cherry and pear trees, the canopy of leaves allowing only soft filtered sunlight through.

"I love coming out here." Dad put his hands on his hips and looked around. "It's so peaceful, at least when it's empty. I don't come out here when they're picking unless I have to."

Adam laughed. "Yeah, I'll bet harvest time isn't exactly quiet."

"It's energizing, really. I love knowing that so much good stuff is coming out of here, but I don't think the guys like having me wander around watching them work. When it's empty, though, there's almost no place I'd rather be."

He looked around him, taking in the quiet beauty as they walked among the trees. The grass was soft under his feet, bees buzzed lazily around flowers, and he knew his dad was right. He never appreciated it as a boy; he'd always balked at the strenuous chores and daydreamed about getting out from under the weight of his family's name. He'd spent many hours picking pears out here, and the orchard wasn't near the size then that it was now. He'd picked tea, planted seeds, mowed grass, everything. Adam couldn't romanticize the back-breaking labor that went into making it all happen, but the magic of nature was something to behold. They made small talk as they wandered through the orchard, and he could tell that something more was on his father's mind.

He knew better than to pry; they would talk when Dad was ready. He just hoped that was soon, before they were again surrounded by others, whether it was his brothers or farm employees, or customers. Richard Whitman was a fixture in Emerald Springs and was rarely alone.

"Have you seen your brothers since you got here?"

"Actually, yes. They stopped by last night when you were out." He let his eyes wander around the orchard, wondering how much trouble it would be to start producing honey. They could market it along with the pears and cherries, sell to local businesses, and add it to their always-growing line of tea products.

"That's good. I don't want to monopolize your visit and keep you from catching up with everyone." Was Adam mistaken or was that a meaningful look? It would be just like Emerald Springs for Dad to have already heard that he and Zoe went out for drinks.

He looked away, not sure if he wanted to get into his renewed, and unwise, interest in her. He'd never kept much from his father, though, and the truth was that nothing had happened. And nothing would happen between them. Too much had gone wrong, and he had a job and life to get back to. "They were waiting for me when I got home from taking Zoe out for drinks."

He trained his eyes on the tree line and stuffed his hands in his pockets. Zoe was so enmeshed in the Whitman family, he couldn't predict how they would react to his spending time with her. Surely they'd grown protective of her in his absence. He could guess that Chad and Daniel—his own father, too—would discourage her from getting close to him unless he was going to stick around.

But his dad only regarded him with an amused look. "Oh yeah? Well, that certainly didn't take long."

"Nothing happened. We shared a pitcher of beer and caught up, that's it." Adam stopped himself before he rambled.

"And the flowers, was that nothing too?" His father raised his eyebrows and kept the maddening amused look on his face.

"I'm almost afraid to ask how you know about that." He grinned despite himself.

"Kathleen called me, all excited that you were in town and wondering what was going on between you two. I didn't know what to tell her." He laughed. "You know there are no secrets in this town."

"I should have known it was Kathleen. I ran into Marlon Miller on the street and ducked into her shop after I saw him just to get away. I couldn't very well stop in there and leave empty-handed."

Dad let out a low whistle. "Marlon Miller, huh? What a piece of work. Did Zoe see him?"

"Yeah, he was on his way to her shop when I passed him. I picked her up after he left."

"How did she seem to you after she saw him?" His dad's expression was one of genuine concern. That Marlon continued to drink despite his doctor's warnings was the worst-kept secret in town.

"Well, she finished most of the pitcher we shared, if that tells you anything. I got the impression he pretty much just stops by to hit her up for money. She was kind of rattled when I got there." It was strange to talk about Zoe so openly after years of carefully avoiding even saying her name.

"She really got a bum deal with those parents. It's a wonder she turned out so well." He shook his head and kicked at the dirt beneath his feet.

"Yeah, not everyone gets the idyllic childhood I enjoyed."

"You and your brothers don't know how good you have it." His father squinted into the soft sunlight.

"We do know, Dad. Believe me."

"All right, then, don't get all mushy. Let's head up to the facilities and I'll show you the new equipment."

They bumped along in companionable silence as the golf cart rolled down the path toward the facilities buildings. This time they parked in front of a nondescript building that housed the withering room.

The pocket of warm, fragrant air that hit Adam as he entered was as familiar as everything else at the farm, but he wasn't prepared for the sheer size of the facility. The old operation was nothing compared to this enormous new space. Growing up, he had worked in the withering room plenty of times, had spent hours spreading leaves evenly on the trays in the warm air of the fans. He'd complained his way through hours of processing without ever appreciating the care his father insisted go into the family's product. Thousands of tea leaves sat in the warm air, losing moisture so they would be prepared for the next step. They'd be moved to rolling belts next, where the leaves would twist into wiry shapes before being laid out to oxidize. Then they'd finally move on to the drying room, where the tea would be passed under hot air dryers to stop oxidation and complete the process.

As a teen, Adam had spent plenty of time helping his family create and test new flavored blends, adding dried fruits and spices to the finished tea. He'd packaged the teas and delivered them to local businesses when the farm was just starting out. Now Emerald Tea was a national brand, and he could see the same attention to craft went into every batch. It was humbling, seeing his father continue to care so much about the tea from start to finish.

"It's really something, isn't it?" Dad broke the silence.

"It's incredible. It's hard to believe that this is the same place I used to live, the same things I used to do."

"Things have really changed as we got bigger. I'll tell you, farming is a lot easier now." he joked.

"Only because you don't have to do any of it any more, right?" Adam nudged his father with his elbow.

"Yep. It's amazing how much work gets done now that I've hired a staff full of younger, stronger people to do all the heavy lifting." He stretched and looked around the withering room, clearly enjoying the result of his life's work.

"So why retire then? Aren't you still enjoying it?"

"I love it. The business has outshone any expectation I ever had for it. It's my legacy, and of all the family businesses, it's the one I'm most proud of. The restaurant and resort are wonderful, but the farm feeds everything else. The farm is the only thing I ever started that literally had to be grown by seed and nurtured by hand." His dad looked thoughtful. "I'm not a young man, though. I want to make plans for the future before I'm too old to see them through. I want to do things my way, not wait so long to retire that decisions have to be made for me."

"Have you thought about what you want for this place?"

"Of course. I would love to see the brand continue to grow and come out with new blends, and at the same time I want it to stay in the family. We can sell it any day of the week; there are always interested buyers. But I don't want some big corporation swooping in and lumping the tea in with all the other products they sell."

"Have you thought about working out a joint management situation between Chad and Daniel? I know they are each busy with the other businesses, but maybe if they knew how much it meant to you, they'd try to figure something out." He was treading into dangerous territory, and if he wasn't careful he'd talk himself into taking the job himself. Why couldn't he leave well enough alone?

Dad opened his mouth and then closed it, shaking his head slightly. Adam had clearly said the wrong thing. All of the Whitman men had each, in their own ways, accused him of discounting the importance of the family businesses, of minimizing the focus required to run it. He held up his hands defensively.

"Never mind. It was just a thought. I'm ready to sit down for a serious conversation, really find out what I'd be in for. I can't hang around here, just thinking about it. I need to know what I'd be signing on for, exactly what you need from me, and then I can make an informed decision."

"Great. I'd like for you to spend some time in the office, get you involved with the big issues facing the business right now. Let me take you by the new storage building, or I guess more like the showroom since Ashley got her hands on it, and then we'll set up a time. Let's get out of here. Your mother always worried that talking too much around the withering trays ruined the teas. She said it was the carbon dioxide, but I think she was just tired of all my hot air."

They squinted in the sunshine as they adjusted to being outdoors again. Adam enjoyed the light breeze that blew past them after being ensconced in the drowsy warmth of the building. Instead of hopping onto the cart, this time they walked the short distance to the stock building.

Ashley Whitman was chatting with a woman in a cream pantsuit, their blonde heads bent over a clipboard Ashley was holding, when they walked in. A wide smile spread across Ashley's face when she noticed them. She placed a hand on the other woman's arm and excused herself before running over to them as fast as her stiletto heels would carry her.

"Adam! I heard you were in town. It's so good to see you." She pulled him into a tight hug and squeezed.

"Good to see you, too, Ash. Working hard?" He hadn't seen his cousin since Christmas, but the woman waiting for Ashley's attention was clearly there on business. This was no time for a family reunion.

"Always. Adam Whitman, this is Caroline Quick. She owns Coffee Queen, and we're talking about how Emerald teas can fit in with her business."

He shook the woman's hand. "Great to meet you, Ms. Quick." He briefly wondered if his Uncle Sam would be resentful if he stopped by and saw the woman who bought his failing business shopping for Whitman products.

"It's so nice to meet you, but please, it's Caroline. No need to be so formal." Was she fluttering her eyelashes?

"All right, Caroline it is," he said, enjoying her reaction to his attention despite himself.

"Wait, Adam Whitman?" She pointed to Ashley and back to Adam. "Are you two ... ?"

"We're cousins," said Ashley. "Emerald Tea Farm has grown by leaps and bounds in the last decade, but at its core, it's a family business. This is my uncle Richard. He is the founder and heart of the operation." Ashley was clearly shifting back into professional work mode, obviously keeping her mind on the deal she was working to close.

Caroline extended her hand to Richard and gave him the same flirtatious look she had given Adam. "Wow, another handsome Whitman man."

"I haven't been in Coffee Queen since before Uncle Sam sold it. Have you made any major changes?" Adam wondered if the diner and Zoe's bakery were still different enough to peacefully coexist on the same street.

Caroline looked pleased by his interest. "I love the interior, the classic diner feel of the place, so that hasn't changed. Much of the menu is the same, since honestly a lot of our regular diners expect their usual dishes. I've been expanding a bit to reflect the tastes of our more health-conscious patrons, adding more healthy options made with fresh local ingredients, things like that."

"Which is where Emerald Tea Farm products fit in perfectly," Ashley interjected. Adam thought she might be hinting for them to leave she could focus on her deal.

"Absolutely. You can't go wrong with tea," Adam agreed.

"Are you planning on joining us for family dinner tonight?" Ashley asked Adam.

"I wouldn't miss it." He smiled at being right—she was definitely ready for them to leave.

"Great, I'll see you then. I can't wait to catch up." Ashley steered Caroline away from them and toward a work table.

Adam turned to his dad and said, "I think we've been dismissed."

"I think you're right. I've got some things to work on this afternoon, so let's catch up at dinner. See you over there at six, sound good?"

"Sure, I'll be there," he said, and left his father to head back to the house. He'd call the office to check on the Everlight Optics deal and spend some time reviewing the promotion offer before it was time to meet the family, and of course Zoe, for dinner. With his father out of the house all afternoon, it would be a great time to check his email and finally give some attention to the packet of information on his promotion offer. The farm and his family were already pulling him toward giving in and staying in town. Perhaps looking over the benefits and compensation package Eco Initiatives was willing to offer him would quell those desires.

Chapter Five

Zoe closed the refrigerator and untied her apron as she headed from the kitchen to the front of the shop. She hung her apron on a hook and stopped by the cash register to chat with Courtney before they closed up for the evening.

"Can you lock up? I want to freshen up a bit before dinner tonight." She attempted a casual tone, but Courtney likely knew exactly what was going on.

Courtney winked and gave her a mischievous grin. "I thought it was just family dinner."

"It is just family dinner, but that doesn't mean I don't want to look nice." She bumped her with her hip and decided to make light of the situation. Courtney was teasing her, but it was good-natured.

"Does this have anything to do with a certain hot out-of-town visitor joining you guys tonight?" She waggled her eyebrows comically.

"Can't a girl just put on a little lipstick without getting the third degree?" She rolled her eyes and watched as Courtney zipped up the bank bag.

"I'm just teasing you. Of course I can take care of everything here." Courtney locked the front door and turned the sign to CLOSED. "I'll make the deposit, and you take the rest of the evening for yourself. Have a great time; all this stuff will be here in the morning." She waved her hand around the bakery, which was already mostly in order for the next business day.

"Thanks, Court. I owe you one." She left out the side door and made her way upstairs to her apartment above the bakery. She hummed to herself as she fished her keys out of her pocket and checked her watch. She had enough time to shower and actually do something with her hair before she had to be across town at Emerald Eats. With any luck, nobody would comment on how she usually looked on family dinner nights—like she'd just left work, which she had. It had been ages since she put any effort into her appearance, but her unexpected reaction to seeing Adam again had put her so off balance, she needed any advantage she could get. He'd probably look fresh and amazing, so she didn't want to look like she'd spent all day in a hot kitchen.

She stepped into the shower, sighing with pleasure as the warm water washed away the day's work. Closing her eyes as she lathered shampoo into her dark hair, her mind drifted to the night before. After so many years apart, she had finally reached the point where she could think about Adam without yearning for their past. It had been much more difficult at first, when she saw him in everything and everywhere around her. But the Whitmans were her family; they were who she turned to in times of sadness, who celebrated with her when she triumphed. She sometimes forgot Richard and Sheila weren't her parents since they were the ones who had always been there for her when her own parents were more like unruly teenagers than responsible caregivers. Spending time alone with Adam again brought back feelings she thought were long buried. She wasn't prepared for her body to betray her by reacting instantly to the mere sight of him by craving more of his touch. The gentle warmth of his hand on the small of her back made her pulse race; what would she do if he actually held her in his arms? She rinsed out her hair and reminded herself that she wouldn't find out. He'd be on a plane back to his life and work in Los Angeles before she knew it, and life would return to normal.

Steam followed her as she stepped out of the shower and wrapped herself in a thick, white towel before wandering through her apartment to her bedroom. She stood in front of her closet and considered her choices, mentally discarding every other outfit before choosing a turquoise dress that complimented her eyes and showed off her legs. She pulled the dress over her head and pushed her feet into a pair of cute kitten heels before starting on her makeup. There was no harm in spending a little extra time on her appearance tonight.

Satisfied with her look, she tucked her wallet and lip gloss into a handbag and headed out the door. As she locked up behind her, shouting from the street below reached her ears. The familiar voice sent a chill of dread through her body, and she ignored the instinct to simply lock herself back in the apartment. She pulled her cell phone out of her handbag, just in case, and took the stairs down to the street. The shouting got louder as she got closer, and with every step she considered turning around and heading for the parking lot behind the building. It would be easier to get in her little car and speed off across town than to confront what she was sure waited for her around the corner. Courtney was likely still inside the bakery, though, and the angry voice outside was accompanied by the sound of pounding fists on the glass door. As much as she wanted to retreat, she couldn't in good conscience leave her assistant alone to handle the confrontation, regardless of the bile that rose in her throat . . .

Her legs propelled her, almost against her will, toward her father. He was pounding on the door of her shop and shouting, oblivious to the stares of passersby or his daughter approaching.

"Dad," she said with a raised voice as she put her hand on his arm.

He whipped around, and the sour smell of sweat and alcohol hit her. "Where have you been? I've been out here forever." His words were slurred and his eyes were bloodshot.

"What are you doing here, Dad?" She kept her tone gentle, though she wanted to shout, to shake him, and demand that he sober up.

"I was having drinks with my friends, down there," he said as he pointed down the street to The Rusty Tap. "It's my turn to buy a round, but I lost my wallet. Or I left it at home, or someone stole it. Maybe it was you." He jabbed a finger at her, and she flinched. "Where's my wallet?"

"I don't have your wallet. Is that it?" She pointed to a bulge in his shirt pocket. He slapped a hand to his chest and felt it.

"All right, I guess you didn't steal it." His eyes still squinted suspiciously, and she lost her patience with him.

"Why don't I drive you home? You can pick up your car tomorrow." She put a hand on his back and tried to push him in the direction of her car.

He shrugged away from her so swiftly, he stumbled a few steps before righting himself. He pulled himself up until he was standing straight, and sniffed. "I'm fine, and I don't need my kid to take care of me," he said with exaggerated dignity. "I'll make my own way home."

She gave up; she wasn't going to chase her father down the street and wrestle him to the ground. He crossed the street, and she held her breath until he safely reached the other side. It would be just her luck that she'd let him go only to have him get himself run over right in front of her. He wove his way down the sidewalk until he disappeared into the bar, and she remembered that Courtney might still be in the bakery. Afraid her employee would see her standing there, a silent witness to Zoe's humiliation, she turned and looked into her shop. She breathed a sigh of relief when she saw that it was empty inside. Courtney must have left just before her dad arrived. At least she was saved from that embarrassment.

Feeling like she should do more but just as certain he wouldn't accept any interference from her, Zoe walked to her car. After buckling herself in, she sat for a moment, taking time to calm down and shift her attitude before joining the Whitmans for dinner. Her father's behavior was no secret, but she wasn't in the mood to air her dirty laundry when Adam was in town. If she could just hold on to her sanity until after he went back home, she could stop by and have tea with Richard and Patty. They always made her feel better, reminding her that it wasn't her fault her father was a disappointment and a drunk. If she could just keep it together a few more days, everything would fall into place.

She started the car and found a classic rock station on the radio, cranked it up, and pulled out of the parking lot. The air conditioner's cold air blew in her face, cooling both her body and her mood. It was time to relax with the family that took her in and forget about the troubles brewing with the family she'd come from. She zipped down the city streets on her way to the restaurant and left her cares behind , feeling better, lighter, with every passing minute.

•••

Chairs scraped against the floor and conversations buzzed through the air as the Whitmans settled into their seats along the two tables Chad had pushed together for them in the corner of Emerald Eats. Adam strode through the early evening crowd, a wide smile on his face, until he reached Chad and Daniel.

"We thought for sure you'd be back on a plane heading home already." Chad ribbed him.

"Yeah, hope we're not keeping you from saving the world," Daniel joked.

"Keep it up, guys. You'll miss me when I'm gone." Adam grinned at his brothers, glad to be home.

"Yeah, yeah, we know. Hey," Daniel lowered his voice and looked to the table. Seeing their father in conversation with Patty, he frowned and continued. "Have you talked to Dad about the farm yet? He has been obsessing over the future lately."

Adam lowered his head. "Well, yeah, that's the main reason I came up. We spent a few hours out on the farm this morning, but we haven't had a chance to talk in detail about his plans. Are you worried about it?"

Chad moved in and huddled with his brothers. "He's stuck on the idea of keeping the farm in the family, but he doesn't seem interested in discussing how we can work it out with the restaurant and resort to worry about." He moved a finger between himself and Daniel. "We've offered to spend some time working out a plan so he doesn't have to leave it in the hands of an outsider, but he thinks our attention would be too divided."

"You know, to be fair, if you're never going to consider coming home, you need to tell him," Daniel added. "I get the feeling he's holding out hope you'll come in and take over. He's always wanted you to take his place."

Adam glanced over at the table. "I might be convinced to consider it. I'm just not sure if it would be the right move to quit my job so I can come back here to be a farmer."

Chad leveled him with an uncharacteristically serious look. "Is that what you think of Dad? Of us? You've been out there. It's a huge enterprise, in case you haven't noticed, not the same little tea farm you worked on as a kid. Don't be so condescending."

"I didn't mean it like that. My job in L.A. is really taking off, and I don't know if I want to leave it behind. If I come home, I lose all that momentum, all the years of work I've put in, and someone else will take my position. It's a big decision, that's all."

Daniel raised an eyebrow. "We know what you mean. Don't worry; nobody's going to ask you to do anything you don't want to do. I just think you need to make sure Dad knows you have no intention of coming back if that's the case. He needs to let that go and move on."

"I'll talk to him, and if I definitely decide not to move back to Emerald Springs, I'll try to help him figure something out. Don't worry." Adam looked toward the door. "Isn't Zoe coming tonight?"

"She's usually right on time," said Chad.

Adam turned back to his brothers only to see them grinning at him like fools. "What? I'm just concerned."

"Sure you are," said Daniel with a laugh. "I'm sure she'll be here soon. She probably got caught up baking muffins or something."

Either he was transparent or his brothers were more perceptive than he gave them credit for. It was such dangerous territory, seeing her so often when he was in town for such a short time. Nothing good could possibly come from it; they weren't going to mend their broken relationship, and interacting with her certainly wasn't making it any easier to squash his reignited feelings for her. Whatever he told himself over the last several years, he was wrong. Distance and time had done nothing to dull his feelings for her. The sooner he worked through his family business and got out of town, the better. At least when he was in Southern California and away from Zoe, he could tell himself that he didn't miss her. He could immerse himself in work and distract himself from everything he had left behind; pretend he didn't want it back.

"Let's go sit down. Ashley looks bored out of her mind." Chad tilted his head toward their cousin, who was sitting at the table between her father—their Uncle Sam—and their dad. His head was bent toward Patty, oblivious to the rest of the restaurant, and Sam was staring off into space.

The three Whitman brothers took seats at the table. Adam was both glad and embarrassed they had left the last open chair next to him for Zoe. They chatted with Ashley, and soon they fell into the familiar rhythms that were never forgotten, no matter how many miles separated them. A pretty blonde waitress approached the table.

"Now I can tell just by looking that you're a Whitman. You must be Adam." He nodded, and his brothers laughed. "I've heard all about you. What can I get everyone to drink?" The waitress pulled a pencil and pad of paper from her apron pocket. She wrote down the drink orders, and looked to the head of the table. "Is Zoe coming tonight, Mr. Whitman?"

"She should be here any minute. Can you bring her an iced green tea?" his dad asked. "Thank you."

Adam was struck again by how enmeshed Zoe was in his family and how separate from everyone else he had become. Was there a way to return to the fold when you were the one who created the divide? UCLA had been his ticket out. A part of him sometimes considered coming back to use his training in environmental sciences to further develop the family businesses, but if he were honest with himself, he never truly intended on living here again. Seeing Zoe made him wonder if it might be time to reevaluate, though. He was lucky she was willing to speak with him at all after he'd dismissed their relationship so thoughtlessly. Was there any possibility she would give him another shot? Why was he even wondering?

As though answering his thoughts, Zoe breezed through the door and made her way through the restaurant, waving to the family as she arrived. For Adam, time stopped for a moment. No matter how many years they were apart, he'd never find anyone who affected him like she did. She hooked her purse over the back of the chair next to him and sat, smoothing her dress beneath her. He tore his eyes away from her legs and greeted her along with everyone else, struggling to act normal.

"I'm sorry I'm late, got caught up at work." She was breathless. And breathtaking.

"Was there some kind of éclair emergency?" Ashley teased.

Zoe laughed and scooted her chair closer to the table. "Something like that." She turned to Adam, and his throat tightened. "Hey," she said, her voice low and sweet.

"Hey," he choked out. If he didn't snap out of it, he'd make a complete fool of himself before dinner was over. He glanced up and saw his father watching him, an amused smile on his face as he nudged Patty, who glanced up and smiled knowingly.

The waitress appeared with a tray of drinks and passed them out. "What's everyone having tonight?" she asked and pulled her pencil and pad out again.

Adam studied the menu, impressed with the offerings. He'd never noticed in the past, but Chad had done an excellent job with the restaurant. When his parents opened Emerald Eats, it was a cozy diner that offered simple dishes made with local produce. Under Chad's direction, the little diner had grown into a chic café with sophisticated dishes. It was still an organic farm-to-table restaurant, and most of the ingredients used were grown at the Whitman farm, another testament to his family's commitment to good environmental stewardship. It was no wonder Adam had gone into environmental sciences. How could he choose anything else after growing up steeped in the traditions of organic farming? He ordered a veggie sandwich and sat back to enjoy the conversations pinging back and forth.

His head was swimming as he took in the atmosphere around the table. In so many ways, nothing had changed, yet at the same time, everything was different. It was strange to sit there as a visitor, knowing that every other week this scene played out without him. And then there was Zoe. Many times over the last seven years, he had wondered if ending their relationship had been the right thing. When they'd reunited five years ago after his mother died, everything with her felt so perfect, but he'd let their relationship slip through his fingers again when he left her in Emerald Springs and ran back to L.A. Being with her colored everything else in his life. Though he tried to find the right woman for his new life, nobody quite fit the bill. Even those who were perfect on paper always seemed to fall short. It was so easy to tell himself he'd made the right decision when he never saw Zoe, never heard from her.

Now he wasn't so sure. Having her beside him, blending seamlessly with his family, felt so right that his chest actually ached.

He turned to Zoe and watched as she chatted with his cousin. She was animated, describing some bakery mishap, and he was sure he'd never seen anyone more delectable. She noticed him watching her and turned to face him, her blue eyes almost turquoise in the light. She raised an eyebrow, as though challenging him to say something. He had her attention, now what?

He lowered his head so that his lips were almost touching her ear and whispered, "You look beautiful tonight."

Zoe sat back a bit, an indecipherable look on her face. He'd said the wrong thing. She wasn't some random girl who'd be flattered by the attention. He couldn't just feed her sweet words and expect her to fall into his arms. He knew better, so why had he said that?

"I didn't mean to embarrass you. Sorry," he said quickly, dismissing the compliment.

"It's okay; I just wasn't expecting it. Thanks," she finished weakly. The waitress arrived at their table, and Zoe went slack with relief as she accepted her glass of tea. He couldn't help but stare as she sipped through a straw, her lips pursed prettily. It would be so easy to lean over and kiss her, and it was almost irresistible. He had to stop; he wouldn't make it through dinner if he kept thinking about those lips.

He turned to his uncle and cousin. "Dad showed me around earlier, and I love what you guys have done with marketing. I didn't get a chance to tell you earlier, but it's really something." Sam was head of marketing for Emerald Tea Farm, though Ashley was more likely to be on site with her hands in the business.

"Thanks. Ashley deserves all the credit, though. She's had a lot of great ideas lately. I've been concentrating more on the operations side and letting her get more involved with marketing." Sam sat back in his chair, looking satisfied.

Adam shot a glance at his father, who shook his head almost imperceptibly. Sam Whitman was head of marketing—why would he concentrate on operations? Was he still harboring fantasies of taking over when Dad retired? He recalled a huge argument over Christmas dinner a few years back when his father made it clear that Sam wasn't in line to take over after his retirement, that he intended the farm to go to one of the boys. Chad and Daniel must have been more definitive lately in their refusal to take the helm; Sam would have sensed an opportunity.

Adam changed the topic, ready to move on to something less controversial. "Ash, I was at Zoe's bakery and she filled me in about the work you guys are doing for the Senior Day Center."

Ashley swallowed the tea she was drinking and nodded. "Yep, although they do the great work; we just bring the goodies."

"I think it's wonderful, and you two should be proud of yourselves," he gestured to include Zoe in the conversation.

She smiled, pleased, and looked much more comfortable than with his previous compliment. "It really is nothing. I want to give back to the community, and this is an easy way to do it."

"Well, sure, giving back is great, but it's not like anyone expects you to go above and beyond like that."

"Why not? A lot has been given to me, you know. I wouldn't even have my bakery if it weren't for your dad, and I doubt your family businesses would be as successful as they are without the support of the community." She sat back while the waitress put her plate in front of her, smiling up at her gratefully.

"What do you mean? What does Dad have to do with your bakery?" He looked down the table to see his dad accepting his meal from the waitress.

"I'll let Zoe fill you in on the details if she wants to," his dad cut in, "but yeah, I fronted the money for her shop, just like I'd do for any of you kids. She had a solid business plan, and it was a good investment. She was successful enough to pay it all back with no trouble."

Surely that announcement would draw some attention, but no. Everyone was tucking into their dinners and not at all surprised by the news. To them, Zoe was as much a part of their family as he ever was. She didn't need him by her side to belong to the Whitmans; she had been there all along. He turned to her and raised his eyebrows. She finished a bite of pasta and dabbed her lips with her napkin. "What? Did you want me to call you up and discuss it with you?" she practically snapped at him. "It's a long story, but the gist of it is that I got a small business loan to open the bakery and was unable to make my payments when my ex-boyfriend drained the bank account and skipped town. Your dad was kind enough to help me, and it was lucky I made enough to pay him back. I don't think I could show my face around town if I had stiffed him."

His dad finished the bite he was chewing and looked at Zoe fondly. "You were a good bet, sweetheart. I never doubted you could do it."

She cast her eyes down at her plate, obviously flattered. "Thank you. Your faith in me helped get me through a really rough time."

"Honey, if your shop ever closed its doors, who would bake my favorite cherry coconut cookies?" he teased.

She laughed. "You know I'd make those for you whether or not I had the bakery."

"I couldn't take the chance." His dad put a hand to his heart and swooned dramatically, causing Patty to giggle and gaze up at him. Daniel shot her an irritated look, and Adam made a mental note to ask him about it later.

So Dad had bankrolled Zoe's bakery? It was becoming more obvious as the night wore on that she was a Whitman, regardless of her last name. And this boyfriend? How did he drain her account?

"What happened to the boyfriend? Is he in jail?" He ignored the jealousy rearing its head at the thought of her with another man and focused instead on the wrongdoing.

The look she shot him could only be described as withering. "It was a joint account, so no, he's not in jail. He took the money and left me. There wasn't much I could do about it since the money was as much his as it was mine." She spared him the eye rolling, but her tone made it clear she thought he was hopelessly egotistical if he assumed she'd been pining away and waiting patiently for him to return to her this whole time.

A joint account. Wow. Logically, Adam knew she would have dated other guys after him. Hell, she could have married someone else by now. So being surprised that she had someone important enough to share a joint bank account with was crazy. He didn't really expect that time stopped when he broke up with her, did he? Fortunately, Chad changed the subject so Adam could stop stewing over his loss.

"I have several new dishes I'm thinking of adding to the menu. Anybody available for a little taste test tomorrow evening?" Everyone at the table declined, citing different reasons.

"I could come by," Adam offered, and on impulse added, "Zoe? Want to join me?"

She swallowed the bite she was eating and cleared her throat. Her eyes were wide, almost panic-stricken, and he wondered if she'd come up with a quick excuse. "Um, sure. I guess I could meet you up here."

"No need. I'll pick you up after work."

And just like that, he had scheduled another date with her.

Chapter Six

Adam and Zoe walked into Emerald Eats, into the noise of an early dinner crowd, and wound their way across the restaurant to a booth in the corner. He slid into the seat across from her and, moving the table's menus to the side, he leaned forward and said, "I guess we won't need menus if Chad wants us to try new dishes. I hope you don't mind being his guinea pig."

"Not at all. It actually sounds like fun."

Chad approached them, pausing a few times as people they knew stopped him to chat. Finally he reached them and leaned over their table. "Hey guys. I'm sending over a couple of half-portions of the new items so you can try a bit of everything. Sound good?"

"Sounds perfect. I'm starving," she said.

"Great, then you two enjoy dinner, and I'll stop by later to see what you thought." He tapped out a rhythm on the table and left, already on to the next task in his busy evening.

"He seems to be doing really well lately."

"Yeah, I'm glad he's found his niche. I'm really impressed with what he's done with this place. Remember how different it used to be?" Adam leaned forward, and light glinted off the face of his Rolex, Richard Whitman's traditional college graduation gift to his sons.

"I know! It was like coming over to eat at your grandma's house when it first opened. I wouldn't recognize it if I hadn't been here to see the changes take place." She smiled and shook her head.

A waitress arrived with a couple of glasses of iced tea and an appetizer for them to share. He thanked her and proceeded to study the beige dip, pieces of roasted garlic dotting the surface.

"Do you think this is new? It seems like hummus would be on the menu already."

"I've never had it here." She dipped a triangle of warm flatbread into the mixture and tasted it, closing her eyes as she chewed. "Mmm. This is delicious, but you might regret bringing me here when you get a whiff of my garlic breath later." Not that it mattered, since their lips wouldn't be mingling any time soon.

He tasted the hummus and grinned at her as he swallowed his bite. "We'll cancel each other out."

"I didn't realize how hungry I was," she said after finishing her bite. "It was so busy today that I didn't get a chance to eat lunch."

"I guess when you're working on your feet all day, snagging a pastry out of the case doesn't really cut it, huh? Must have been crazy over there if you couldn't find a few minutes to eat in the back or something. Isn't that why you have an employee?"

"Courtney was out sick today, so it was just me. It used to always be just me before I could afford to hire her, but I forgot how hard it was to not get a break."

"She's your only employee?"

"Yeah. I've been toying with the idea of hiring someone new, maybe a part-time position. I don't think she ever intended to work full-time with me, and that would take some of the pressure off. When she can't come in, it's so hard. It's just not a one-person job any more."

"That's impressive, you know, to start a small business on your own and find yourself in the position to hire employees so soon. The bakery must be doing really well."

"It is. It feels like I've put a million hours into it, but I wouldn't change a thing."

The waitress arrived and placed two large platters between them and gave them each a clean dinner plate. They settled into a comfortable silence as they sampled entrees and side dishes that didn't necessarily go together: vegetable enchiladas alongside herbed potatoes, pear and gorgonzola salad with garlicky stuffed mushrooms, but were delicious nonetheless. The temptation to keep things light and flirty was strong, but with their history, things would never be casual between them.

"So, at the risk of ruining the whole evening, I'm going to ask something. It's been killing me, and I have to know. What's the story with this other boyfriend?" He took a bite of an herbed potato dish and chewed while he waited for her reply.

She sipped her drink, considering her answer. "How much do you want to know? It's been over for a while and I haven't dated anyone seriously since him."

"I guess it's none of my business, but I'm curious about him. If you two were serious enough to live together, I imagine things were moving forward. Had you planned on getting married?"

"He never asked, and I never brought it up. I guess by that point, I was a little gun shy about asking for a commitment."

"What do you mean?"

"Well," she squirmed in her seat, "it was after your mom passed away, after we, you know … " When he was in town for his mother's funeral, Adam and Zoe had turned to each other for comfort and ended up in a bittersweet, ill-advised fling. Before she had time to decide if getting back together was a good idea, he was back in L.A. and out of her life, ending things with an abrupt phone call.

"Oh."

"So, at that point, I guess I was ready to move on, and I jumped into the relationship. I didn't feel like I could push him for a real commitment. You know, seeing how that backfired on me before."

He was quiet for a moment, his blue-green eyes serious. "You and I," he tilted his fingertips back and forth between them, "didn't work out back then, but it wasn't because you pushed for a commitment."

"I realize that now, but at the time, it really felt like I should do whatever I could to hold onto the relationship. I was scared to risk pushing him away and ending up alone again. It was stupid, but that was a confusing time for me. I'm almost glad I went through that, though, because it forced me to grow up. I'm not the same person I was back then, and it's because of that experience."

He swallowed hard, his Adam's apple bobbing in his throat. She was happy and well-adjusted now, but she'd been through some dark times, and he was responsible for some of it. His cavalier attitude had done more damage than she would ever admit to him.

"Life can really knock you on your ass, sometimes, huh?"

She had to laugh at that. "Yeah, I guess you could say that. It's fine, really, and I'm fine. Like I said, I'm not the same person anymore. Being on my own has forced me to grow, to take responsibility for my own life. I don't like how things turned out between us, but I haven't carried that pain around with me every day since you left or anything."

"Well, good, I'd hate to think you were carrying a torch for the Whitman kid."

"No worries there. I was pretty committed to Nicholas, even though I think I knew all along he wasn't the one for me. I kept trying to make it work, but it was hopeless. In a way, it wasn't a surprise when he split."

"What? That story surprised the hell out of me."

"Well, the part where he took all of our money and left like a thief in the night was a shock, sure. But I wasn't surprised that it didn't work out."

"So if you didn't think he was the one for you, and you never talked about moving things to the next level, why did you stay with this guy?"

"It seems silly now, but at the time, I was closing in on thirty, and I wasn't sure I would meet someone else if it didn't work out.

I guess I hoped that something would change, that things would somehow click with us."

"You're not exactly an old maid," he said before he took a sip of iced tea.

She leveled him with a serious look. "I'm thirty-two. I know I'm not an old maid, but at the time, I was focused on becoming a mother, and I always thought it would happen by a certain age. I don't know exactly what I want, but at least back then, it seemed important to try to make it work."

"You're nowhere close to being too old to become a mother."

She raised an eyebrow. "I know that, but it still feels like the clock's ticking."

"Okay, but it's not like there's no chance." She wasn't sure if he was trying to convince her or assuage his own guilt. "My parents weren't exactly spring chickens when we were born, and it was great. You're the same age my dad was when I was born, and they had two more after me."

"Sure, there's still a little time, but I don't have any desire to be a single parent, so that means I'd have to find a guy, get married, and then finally have the baby. You see how I might not want to throw away a relationship until I'm sure it's over? I can't just go out and find a single guy. It's not that easy." He cleared his throat. "I'm a single guy." His voice was low, but his meaning was clear.

"Yeah, but I have my doubts about you." She smiled, but it was sad, forced.

• • •

The next day, Adam sat with his father in the business office, sipping on a new tea blend, letting his mind wander as his father gathered files in a neat stack on his desk. When he'd first immersed himself in his new life at Eco Initiatives after college, Adam considered Emerald Springs's slower pace lazy. Now, he wasn't so sure the frenetic pace, the constant meetings necessarily meant things were getting done. One look out the window or a quick glance at his family's bank statements told him that buzz didn't necessarily equal progress. His dad had taken a simple family farm and turned it into a multi-million dollar enterprise, and Adam's brothers were expanding the Whitman legacy. And what had he been doing? Scoffing at their simple lives from his glass and chrome office in a smog-covered city. He was lucky they still claimed him.

"So, do you have any good candidates to take over for you?" Adam asked.

His dad looked up from his work and sat back in his chair. "If you won't do it, I have a few people in mind. Nobody I'm too crazy about, to tell you the truth." He watched Adam carefully.

"And you're sure Chad and Daniel can't work out a way to take on the job together?"

"No. It's not a job that can be handled part-time. The restaurant and resort would suffer, too, and the boys are doing really well right now. Daniel is making the resort his career and I don't want to undermine that. Chad might say yes if I asked, but you know he'd find a way to pass off the responsibility. He just can't commit to something this big. He's been so dedicated to the restaurant lately, and I want to encourage that. They're both really happy doing what they're doing, and they'd only take over the farm out of loyalty." His father looked around the office, pausing to trace his finger along the surface of the desk, so Adam knew he was choosing his next words carefully. "I want someone who will love the farm like I do. I want you to take over, Adam, and I'm tired of putting it off. This is our legacy, son. It's not a job."

Adam's chest constricted as the weight of his father's words hung between them. A rush of guilt leveled him as the gravity of the situation sunk in. If he agreed they should hire someone, it would become just another business, somebody's job. But if Adam took his place at the helm, he could be a part of the Whitman legacy, a part of something that mattered. And Emerald Tea Farm was the backbone not only of the Whitmans' enterprises, but also of Emerald Springs in many ways. He'd lied to himself. Now that the words were out in the open, it did mean something to him.

When Adam pictured a future at the helm of the farm, it felt right, fated even. But could he give up his life in L.A., where he had worked so hard to make a name for himself? The promotion he'd dreamed of for so long he could practically taste it stood between him and this new tug on his heart, and he wished there were an easy answer.

"I know you dismissed it earlier, but what about Uncle Sam?" He scrambled for another solution, not quite ready to give up on exhausting all other avenues.

His dad scoffed. "I love my brother, I really do, but no. He's not cut out for the job and handing over the reins to him would be the end of everything I've ever cared about. He's sloppy, lazy, and to tell you the truth, I don't think he cares one bit if our operations are organic or not. Sam is constantly trying to push fertilizers and treatments that would get our USDA labeling yanked, as though he doesn't realize that being all-organic is half the reason we're so successful."

"But surely he knows the business better than I. It would take me months to get up to speed, when all he'd need to do is get his act together." He was talking over all the possibilities, but it was becoming clear Adam Whitman was the only one who would be right for the job. If only he could decide whether he wanted to accept that or continue to fight to keep things the way they were.

"I've thought about giving him a shot, many times in fact. When he let your Aunt Elizabeth push him into starting Coffee Queen, though, that was the beginning of the end for me, to be honest. Every time he made it clear that he didn't care about his own business, one he started all on his own, I saw how he would potentially handle things if I gave him the farm. The day he decided to sell rather than figure out how to stay afloat was the day I decided there was no way I would take that chance with the farm."

Adam puffed out a short breath. "Wow. I guess I shouldn't be surprised, but I didn't realize how sure you were about him. But I'm still worried about the time it would take for me to get comfortable. It could be months."

"Son, I have months. If you agree to take over, I will be here until you're good and ready to steer this ship on your own. Training you? I can do that. Changing Sam? Not a chance." With that he sat back in his chair and gave a definitive nod of his head. For the first time, he admitted to himself that he could do this. He could picture himself at the helm of Emerald Tea Farm, maybe with Zoe at his side.

"It's really starting to hit me—" They were interrupted by a short knock on the door as it was pushed open.

Sam Whitman stepped in and dipped his head apologetically. "Sorry to interrupt, but the door was open." He gestured for someone to follow him and walked further into the office. "Nobody is at the front right now, so I took the initiative to see our visitor back."

An unfamiliar man who looked to be about Adam's age stepped in, and his father gave him a polite smile. "How can I help you?"

The man crossed the room and extended his hand. "Mr. Whitman? Hi, I'm Alan. I'm new in town, but I've heard wonderful things about Emerald Tea and I was hoping to talk with you about employment opportunities."

Adam couldn't place his accent—was it British? Not quite. Whatever it was, Alan clearly wasn't from around here if his idea of applying for a job was walking into the owner's office and asking for one. As unconventional as this guy's approach was, his father remained unruffled and professional.

"We're actually fully staffed right now, but you're more than welcome to stop by our human resources department and fill out an application. That way we'll have your information on file and can contact you if anything opens up." He stood and gestured toward the door. "I'm sure Sam would be happy to walk you over there."

Sam shot his brother an irritated look, but left anyhow.

The silence played out for a moment after Sam and Alan exited, and then Adam couldn't help it. He laughed. It was just so absurd. "I've been home less than a week, and I've seen the craziest stuff happen around town. What the hell?"

His dad laughed along with him. "I don't know what's going on. Must be something in the air."

"All right, then. I'm going to head out for a bit, try to figure this out. I'm going to give this some serious thought, and I'll have an answer for you within a few days. One way or another, I'll make my decision before this turns into a vacation. We'll talk more later." Adam got up and left his father's office, thinking that life at the helm of Emerald Tea Farm would be more interesting and complex than he'd imagined. Only one thing would stop him, and that was if Zoe closed the door on a future for them. He needed to know if there was any chance they could be together, and there was only one way to find out.

• • •

Zoe counted boxes on her utility shelf, checking off items on her clipboard as she went along. The bakery was warm, fragrant, and quiet this time of day. They expected an after-work rush, but the early afternoon hours were perfect for catching up. She faintly registered the front door bell ringing as a customer entered, but Courtney was in the front. Zoe could stay tucked in the back until they got busier. She heard murmuring and imagined what the customer was choosing. There were cookies, muffins, cupcakes, even a fancy cinnamon pear pastry in the case. No matter how long Everything Nice had been open, she always felt the same flush of pride that so many people enjoyed her baking. She still stood in the middle of the shop and looked around sometimes, amazed that it was all hers, that she'd made a life doing what she loved.

The door opened behind her, and she turned, expecting Courtney. Her expectant look changed to confusion as Adam stood in her doorway, filling the space. She tried for a casual, unsurprised response, but her heart was pounding so hard in her chest, she wanted to hold it in with her hand.

"Hey," she squeaked out. This was ridiculous. How many times had she assured herself that she was good and well over him?

"Zoe," he said, his voice low, deep, and sexy. He crossed the room, his eyes never leaving hers as he walked, confident and with purpose. He stopped in front of her, close enough that she could smell his soap and feel heat radiating from his body. He was so close, too close. "I'm going to kiss you, right now, unless you tell me to stop."

He tipped her face up to his, giving her a moment to decline if she was going to. What was happening? She should say no, she knew it, but the words wouldn't come. She didn't want them to. This was what she'd been missing: all the feelings she'd tucked away and ignored, all the longing she'd denied. It was all here, and his hands on her face brought everything rushing back. He was so serious, but as he lowered his face to hers, a smile spread across his lips. An answering smile crossed her face; she was going to enjoy this. Adam's lips met hers, and fireworks exploded in her head. She returned his kiss and breathed in his familiar but enticing scent as her arms circled his waist and pulled him closer. Without breaking contact, he maneuvered her until her back was to the stainless steel worktable, then picked her up by the waist and set her down gently. The extra height the table gave her made it easier to pull him closer and let her hands wander. Her lips opened beneath his, and he deepened the kiss, his tongue warm and sweet as he explored her. His dark hair was soft under her fingers; she luxuriated in the silky feel of it as his lips and tongue worked their magic on her. Memories, thoughts, and longing zinged through her mind as she gave herself over to the moment. His hands splayed against her back, their warmth sinking through the thin fabric of her t-shirt.

Adam pulled back, though she wasn't ready for the kiss to end. She allowed herself to move forward with him, wishing for another moment of connection. Her eyelids fluttered open, reluctantly, to see him staring down at her with a look of pure masculine satisfaction. The haze of attraction cleared, and her hands flew to her mouth, her eyes wide. What happened to her determination to keep him at arm's length?

"What was that?" she asked, breathless.

"That was amazing." He cupped her face in his hands and laid another soft, sweet kiss on her lips. "I was going to apologize for surprising you, but honestly, I'm not sorry. Not even a little." He grinned down at her and took her hands in his, holding them lightly as she processed his words.

"But why?" As heady as the kiss was, she couldn't fathom why he had barreled in here to lay it on her. They weren't together; he lived in L.A., and this couldn't be good for her. It took long enough to get over him the first two times. How was she supposed to forget now?

"I needed to see if it was as good as I thought it would be between us. And it was," Adam said with a heartbreaking smile.

"Yeah, so?" She attempted a saucy tone, hoping to gain control of her emotions and the situation. Perhaps he wouldn't notice the quiver in her voice.

"So, this changes things. I've been wrestling with some big decisions this week, and I needed to make sure I was right." He nodded decisively.

"Right about what?"

"About us. I kept telling myself that there was no way kissing you would be as good as I imagined, but I was clearly wrong. I needed to see for myself." He shrugged, as though barging into her kitchen and kissing her senseless was a reasonable way to find answers to his questions.

As foolish as it was, excitement surged within Zoe before she carefully tamped it back down with reality. "Oh, really?" she replied archly.

"Oh yeah. I'll pick you up at five tonight. We're going out."

"What if I'm not interested?"

His smile faltered for a microsecond before he recovered. "That kiss said otherwise." He left her sitting on the table and headed toward the door. "Five o'clock," he said as he walked out, triumphantly tapping the top of the doorframe. The door flapped behind him, and she sat alone, wondering what had just happened.

•••

Adam pulled into the driveway at the farm, humming to himself. He tapped a rhythm out on the steering wheel and enjoyed the feeling of the stupid grin on his face before making the walk down to his father's office. Everything was brighter now, if that was even possible. The air was sweet, the birds were singing, and the sun was shining. He was going to take Zoe out and see if there was still something between them worth exploring. This was a good idea—no, a great idea. Why had he avoided it so long? Why did he ever think he'd want to be away from her?

He passed robust fields of tea as he walked to the office, vaguely registering that the workers in the fields were distracted.

Their normal quick, efficient pace seemed off-kilter somehow. He wasn't exactly a regular on the farm, though. It was probably nothing. He let himself in the operations office, a cool blanket of air-conditioned air enveloping him as he entered and greeted the receptionist behind the front desk. She was friendly, if a little distracted. He made his way down the hall to his father's office, only to find it empty. The computer screen glowed, and a pen rested on a notepad with a half-finished sentence. He found his father's assistant and asked where he was, only to be directed down the hall even farther, to the records office.

He found his dad in a meeting with two men in suits, their faces grim, his father's irritated. His dad looked up from the file cabinet where he was extracting folders. "Come on in. These two gentlemen are paying us a visit from Immigration. Apparently someone called in an anonymous tip that we have undocumented workers here."

"What the hell?" He joined him at the file cabinet and lowered his voice. "Is this going to be a problem?"

His father laughed, short and without humor. "It's just an annoyance, not to mention a huge waste of time and taxpayer money." That statement earned a blank look from one of the Immigration officials.

"How can I help?" Adam asked.

"I've just about got everything we need. They'll have to go through the employment records and see for themselves that everyone's legally able to work here. There's no shortcut."

"So you'll leave the files here with them?" Shouldn't they stay and make sure nothing in the investigation was botched?

"Well, sure. I have things to do, and I've already spent the last couple of hours watching these two. They're not going to do anything, not with Arlene sitting right outside the door watching them. She'll keep an eye on things for me." He nodded toward a desk across the hall.

"Wow. You don't seem too worried." He'd always imagined that Immigration officers would cause panic when they arrived on site.

"There's nothing to worry about when you're not doing anything wrong. This isn't the first time we've been visited by Immigration, and I'm sure it's not the last. Whoever called in the anonymous tip must have been awfully convincing," his dad replied before he set a stack of files on a table for the men and told them to let him know when they were finished.

They exited the records room, leaving the door open so the assistant could easily keep an eye on everything. They rounded the corner and slipped into the office; Adam took a seat and his father walked around behind his desk to sit down. Panic crossed his face as he moved items around on his desk, looking for something and growing more frantic every moment. His dad swore under his breath, and the tension in the room ratcheted up.

"What's wrong?" he asked.

"I left a package right here, a large green envelope," he pointed to a spot on his desk. "I swear, I don't remember taking anything with me when the Immigration guys came in." He puffed up his cheeks and let out a breath. "Maybe I did, or maybe the mail guy came by and picked it up by accident. I'll find it."

"Is it important?" The Immigration officials had Adam off-balance already, and now there were missing files?

"A few months ago, another anonymous tipster had the IRS knocking on our door. I had just about cleared everything up with them, and I had one more thing to mail out." He groaned and raked his fingers over his chin. "I've got to find that package."

"Damn," Adam murmured. "What's going on around here?"

"Honestly, I don't know. It could be anything. These two calls could be completely unrelated, or someone could be trying to cause trouble for us."

"Who would do that?"

"It could be anyone—a disgruntled employee, some other business owner. I've thought more than once that it could be Joe."

"Joe Sanders?" His father and Joe had ended their partnership acrimoniously, but it had been twenty years since they went their separate ways. Would Joe still be bitter?

"Yeah, you know, I think at our age we shouldn't be hanging on to old resentments. He has zero interest in reconciling with me, though. He's made that perfectly clear."

"That's too bad. You'd think he would at least be willing to let bygones be bygones. You're practically neighbors." Their farms were separated by nothing more than a fence.

"And if we can't be friends, I thought we could at least move toward being business associates again."

"What do you mean?"

"Rumor has it that Split Acres isn't doing so well. I've been thinking of how we can make an arrangement to buy or lease some of their land that abuts ours. It would be great if we had more room to expand."

"Have you asked him?"

"No, but I've floated the idea out to some of the other guys. I'm sure he's heard about it by now. I haven't been sure how to approach him since he seems so hell-bent on avoiding me." Richard Whitman belonged to a few professional organizations and was in constant contact with other area farmers. Some of them gossiped like teenagers, so it was nearly impossible that Joe hadn't caught wind of his ex-partner's plans by now.

The assistant knocked on the open door and stepped over the threshold. "Sorry to interrupt, but the gentlemen from Immigration are ready to meet with you. Want me to show them to the conference room?"

"Sure, that's fine. I'll be in there in a minute." He pushed his chair back and gathered his notepad and pen even as the assistant disappeared down the hallway.

"This is the kind of nonsense you'll be dealing with if and when you take over for me. Never once in all the years we've been open have we had an issue with employees not having legal status, but it never fails. All it takes is a phone call, and I've got officials swarming in here, combing through the records, looking for something they'll never find. And they always make a mess."

"You handled it pretty well—I mean, it didn't seem to bother you." He chose to ignore his father's comment about taking over the farm.

"It's more of an annoyance at this point, nothing to worry about." He sipped from a glass of water. "You'll get used to it, too."

"Sounds like fun." Adam deadpanned.

"No time like the present. Shall we?" His father patted his shoulder as they approached the records room.

The officials sat, grim-faced, at the table in the records room. "Gentlemen," his father said in greeting.

"Mr. Whitman," the bald one responded.

They sat across from the officials, and Adam watched his father, all traces of humor gone from his face. "So, what was this all about?"

"I'm sorry, but who are you, exactly?" The younger official asked Adam.

"This is my son, Adam Whitman. The next time you get called to paw through our records, he'll be the one in charge." His father's voice rang with authority, and Adam didn't dare interrupt to remind him that he may not become CEO.

"It's good that you're both here, then. First, we'd like to thank you for your cooperation. We realize what an inconvenience these visits can be, but of course you understand that we're just doing our jobs." The bald one gave them a condescending smile.

"And we'd love to get back to ours, so if you don't mind ... " His father spread his hands in front of him.

"Right, well, we came out in response to an anonymous tip our office received questioning the legal work status of some of your employees. We understand that you have seasonal help this time of year, correct?"

"Yes," his father was clearly exasperated. "Tea leaves are delicate and must be picked by hand rather than machine. This time of year, Emerald Tea Farm employs seasonal help to handle the harvest. We've never once had an issue with any employee, seasonal or otherwise, and their legal status to work."

"And you'll be pleased to know that we haven't found any discrepancies," the younger official paused, and smiled. "Yet."

"If you've reviewed the files in response to the complaint, and you've found nothing, then I don't see what more there is to discuss." Adam's blood pressure spiked at the smarmy smile on the official's face. He sat back in the stiff wooden chair and shoved his hands in his pockets, not ready to let the men rattle him.

"In order to conduct a more thorough search of your records, we'll need more time. Farms this size rarely come up squeaky clean when we dig deep enough." The bald official took his glasses off and pulled a small cloth from his pocket to polish the lenses.

His father's jaw clenched and Adam watched his knee bounce. Richard Whitman did everything by the book, and he'd never once run afoul of the law. Adam was shocked the meeting hadn't ended with a handshake and a business card exchange, much less this tense, quasi-threatening conversation. "What are you saying? Do you need to schedule another visit?" Adam kept his tone even, his volume reasonable, but the smirk on the younger man's face threatened to unravel his patience.

"We can call it done," the younger man sat forward, propping his elbows on the table, "and this can all go away."

"Just make it worth our while." The bald, older man replaced his glasses and fixed Adam with a pointed gaze.

Adam pushed to his feet, knocking the chair back behind him, and slammed his fist on the table. Both officials flinched away, identical surprise in their eyes. "Are you threatening me? Or just trying to bribe me?" He bit out the words, lowering his volume, his tone full of fury. "Get out," he almost whispered.

The smirks returned to both the men's faces, and the younger one pushed his chair back and stood. "We can make this easy, or very, very difficult for you." He leaned close to Adam as he finished, close enough for his bitter coffee breath to waft into the space between them.

To stop himself from grabbing the other man by the neck, Adam clenched his hands into fists as he shouted, "Get the hell out of here!"

The younger man finally flinched and stumbled as he moved away from Adam, and the older official hopped to his feet. Neither appeared to grasp his full meaning, so Adam pulled the younger man by the jacket and shoved him toward the door. The bald official scurried after him, clearly worried that he was next. "Arlene!" Adam called to the assistant across the hall. "See these two out, please."

"Mr. Whitman," the older official began.

"We're done," Adam said. "So leave."

He watched as Arlene escorted them out, straightened his shirt, and slowed his breathing. When he finally remembered that his father was still in the room, he went back and picked up the chair he'd toppled, careful to slide it under the table. "Sorry about that, Dad."

His father held up his hands. "Hey, I'm just glad I was able to get out of the way in time."

"I don't know what got into me. I mean, this isn't the first time I've had to deal with scumbags. I never should've put my hands on that guy, but I couldn't stop myself. It was like when he threatened the company, it was personal."

"With this place, business is personal, son. I wish it didn't have to happen this way, but it was actually nice to see you have that reaction."

"You liked that, huh? You would've loved it if I'd gone ahead and done what I really wanted." He mimed a swift uppercut.

"I think that was enough for one day." With his father joking, Adam felt the tension leave his jaw and was able to unclench his fists.

"So now what?" Adam couldn't imagine that the Immigration department would simply drop the matter since he'd sent the investigators away.

"Well, I guess now we wait. If they need to come out again, they will. If the little one wants to press charges over you manhandling him, then lucky for you our attorney is fantastic."

"Damn, I hope it doesn't come to that. I don't want to drag you and the company into some legal problem."

"I'd be surprised to see it come to that, honestly. They'd have to admit that they tried to extort money from us. I'm sure they don't want that to come out."

"True. I guess we'll worry about it when we have to. I've got more pleasant things to concentrate on this evening." Looking forward to seeing Zoe cheered Adam, erased the last remaining tension from his shoulders.

Chapter Seven

Zoe breezed through her bedroom as she finished getting ready, checking herself in the mirror one last time. Everything was perfect; not a hair out of place, her favorite pink dress with the flouncy little skirt was flawless, and her makeup looked good but not too good. Refusing to acknowledge that she'd just spent thirty more minutes than normal getting ready for a date with the ex-boyfriend who broke her heart, she packed her handbag with essentials. Humming to drown out the sensible voice that reminded her how Adam had chosen his life in Los Angeles over her, she focused on the anticipation that strummed through her. Nothing could erase the kiss they shared that afternoon, nothing. That was pure magic—that was Adam and Zoe. A tingle of pleasure zinged through her straight down to her core just thinking about it. Kisses like that could make a girl forget a lot, could lead to some foolish decisions. How bad would it be, really, to get involved with Adam again? After all these years, there was still a connection, something that never went away.

She had been alone a long time, and he had been the only man she'd ever truly loved, the man she measured everyone else against. Seeing him again had brought everything back, like they'd never been apart. Kissing him this afternoon, agreeing to this date, it was scary but what worth having wasn't? It wasn't like he had cheated on her or lied to her; he'd just chosen a different path. She'd been too afraid to follow him on that path then, but there was a chance things could work out now. Zoe wasn't a child; she was a thirty-two-year-old woman who knew what she wanted. If she chose to forget their past and start over, then that's what she would do.

A knock on her door interrupted her internal pep talk, and she took a moment to calm and center herself before greeting Adam.

She would be agreeable tonight but not a pushover. There was no reason he needed to know she hadn't stopped thinking of their kiss. She opened the door and took in his appearance, careful to disguise her initial reaction. He looked good, really good, and her breath hitched despite her stern warning to herself to play it cool. She needn't have worried, though; his eyes were practically smoldering as he stepped in.

"Hey," he said, with a quirk of his lip.

"Hey," she answered, knowing she sounded like a breathy schoolgirl but unable to stop herself.

"So, about that kiss earlier," he began, inching closer. "I haven't been able to get it out of my mind, but now I've told myself it couldn't possibly be as good as I thought."

He came closer, and she felt herself being drawn into his orbit, her eyes closing as their lips met. He pulled her close, one hand on her back, the other cradling the back of her head as it tipped up to meet his. His kiss was firm, hot, and he coaxed her mouth open as she drew in a breath. His tongue pushed into her mouth, tangled with hers, sending a frisson of pleasure skipping all the way down her spine. He tasted minty, warm, and sweet, and more like home than she would have imagined. She let her hands wander across the hard planes of his torso, his body muscled beneath her touch. Knowing what was beneath the clothes made it harder to restrain herself from pulling his shirt out from the waistband of his pants and pushing her hands underneath the fabric. The kiss went on forever, stretching out the moment, and Zoe lost herself in the sensations. All too soon, it was over, and he pulled back, held her face in his hands, and dropped a sweet kiss on her tingling lips.

His eyes were hazy with desire, and his voice was husky when he said, "I didn't think it was possible, but that kiss was even better than the first one." He kissed her forehead, each cheek, and then her lips again before pulling her into an embrace. She could feel his breath on the top of her head, his voice rumbling in his chest. "If we don't leave now, I don't think we will."

She swallowed and nodded her head. He was right; she was one more epic kiss away from dragging him to her bedroom. It would feel so right, but it was so wrong. She couldn't give in to her desires so quickly. "All right then, where are we going?" She ran her fingers through her hair and pulled herself together.

"You'll see," he answered with a playful glint in his eyes. "Ready?" He took her hand and pulled her close for another soft kiss. Before she could melt into his arms, she straightened her spine along with her resolve and grabbed her handbag.

"Let's go." She pulled him out the door and enjoyed the feeling of his hand resting lightly on her shoulder as she locked up her apartment. Safely on the other side of the door, she felt certain she could keep her emotions in check until he gave her a reason to believe he was serious about wanting her back. She hoped.

• • •

Adam parked in front of a little wine bar and turned to Zoe. "Remember this?"

She was adorably confused, looking from him to the building and back again. "Remember what? It's Blush Wine Bar."

"It wasn't always Blush." He watched her, hoping the memory would surface.

Understanding dawned in her eyes. "Ah, yes, I do remember spending endless summer hours inside with a certain Whitman boy back when it was Annie's. Those were some good times, but not exactly what I'd call romantic." Annie's was an arcade when they were growing up, and they never went together as a couple, just as friends when they were kids.

"It's romantic in my mind. I'll always remember Annie's as the place where you went from being that girl from school to the girl of my dreams. It was in there that I fell for you."

The air in the car was charged with energy, and he noticed the space between them growing warmer. "I never knew that," she said softly.

"I think of those days every time I pass this place. You don't want to know what happens when I hear the sound of Pac Man." He grinned as she burst out laughing. "Come on, let's go inside." He hopped out of the car and hurried around to her side to let her out. He took her hand as she climbed out, unable to resist keeping her hand in his as they walked to the restaurant, the soft evening air cool against their faces and sweet with the night's possibilities.

He opened the door for her and guided her with a hand at her side, just where her tiny waist gave way to the soft swell of her hips. The bar's dim lighting and warm atmosphere pulled them in, and they were surrounded by the sound of clinking glasses and soft chatter. They grabbed a booth in a darkened corner and sat across from one another, close enough their knees bumped gently against each other when they moved. She studied the menu, biting her bottom lip as she read. He picked up his own menu to keep himself from leaning across the table and pulling that lip between his teeth, allowing himself instead to indulge in a brief fantasy of how she'd react if he did. She ordered a four cheese and pear pasta dish, and he wondered if the pears came from Emerald Tea Farm. There were so many facets of the business he'd never learned; every time he thought he had a handle on it, something new presented itself, and the possibility of taking over the farm seemed more farfetched. Adam ordered a tortellini pasta dish with sundried tomatoes and a bottle of pinot noir to share.

"So," he said as he sat back in his seat. "Anything interesting happen today?"

Her eyes sparkled with amusement. "No, not really, not unless you count being kissed silly by my crazy ex-boyfriend."

"So now I'm crazy?" He shifted in his seat, warming to the flirtation developing between them.

She shrugged and the moment was broken as the waiter approached with their wine. Adam tasted it and approved, watching her lips and wondering when the next kiss would happen as a glass was poured for each of them. She sipped her wine and sat forward on her elbows, a conspiratorial smile on her face. "So what else do you have planned for us tonight?"

"I have a few surprises up my sleeve. You'll just have to wait and see," he answered. "I already spilled my biggest secret, so the rest are just details."

"What's your biggest secret?" Her lips twitched, and he found himself thinking of tasting them again. Only the server's arrival at that moment broke their eye contact as she put their plates down in front of them.

"That I want to be with you. I didn't admit it even to myself until recently, and now that I have, I feel so much better." He sipped his wine and enjoyed the complex flavors. L.A. had its share of sophisticated restaurants, but Emerald Springs was an underrated bastion of delicious foods and wines. He could be happy here; it was a shame he never thought so before. He'd wasted a lot of time, time he could have spent building a life with Zoe. He tamped down the nagging reminder of the promotion that waited for him on the other end of a plane ride, the only thing stopping him from saying yes to his father. Instead, he'd see where the evening took them.

"You sound pretty sure of yourself," Zoe said.

"Those kisses told me everything I need to know. The rest is just a matter of convincing you it's a good idea." The fact that he'd still have to convince himself to definitely give up the promotion and stay in town was a matter he'd leave for another time.

"So, what made up your mind?"

"I was at the office with Dad today, and some things went down, made me realized how much this place means to me. I don't want to talk about it right now, just want to enjoy the evening with you."

She took a bite of her pasta and glanced around the restaurant. Her neutral expression gave nothing away, and he waited for her to respond. He'd like to have things with her figured out soon, before it was time either to return to work and accept the promotion he'd been gunning for all year, or give his notice and throw himself into learning the family business. She might be tougher to convince than he thought, though, and there was no way he'd consider living in town without her in his life.

She finally swallowed and turned to him, her eyes sad. "It has taken a long time, but I'm fine now. Getting over you was the hardest thing I've ever had to do, and I don't know if I can do it again."

"You won't have to," he said softly. He wouldn't start a relationship with her again if he didn't intend to stick around for the long haul.

"I don't know if I can believe it. I can't close down my shop and leave, and I don't want another long-distance relationship. I know how much you love your job, how much it means to you. I probably didn't really understand it until I opened my own place. That's why it took so long to get over you. It took years, but I was finally happy being on my own, and then you came back and turned me upside down again. Somehow, letting go a second time was even harder." She sipped her own wine and averted her eyes. He could see unshed tears in welling up and wanted to do or say whatever he could to make them go away.

"Back then, I was stupid. I was wrong. I know that now, and I am sitting here telling you it will never happen again. I will not lead you on or start something I don't know if I can finish." He reached across the table and took her hand in his. "I want you. Don't you want to see what we could have together?"

"Wow. I didn't mean for things to get so heavy." She squeezed his hand and extricated hers from his grip to drain her glass of wine. He refilled her glass, never taking his eyes off her expression, looking for a clue that she was softening toward the idea. She was angelic in the restaurant's soft light, and it felt good to have declared his intentions, even if he was still secretly uncertain. The wine must have been working its way through his system, loosening his tension because for the first time in his adult life, he could see himself back in Emerald Springs, at the helm of the family farm, living happily ever after with the love of his life. L.A. and the job that had always meant so much to him seemed both far away and insignificant as he sat across from Zoe. His only regret was that he had waited so long to admit the truth to himself and that he had hurt her in the process.

"Let's order dessert," he suggested. "Unless, of course, you get sick of sweets after working all day."

Her wine-stained lips curled into a sweet smile. "That actually sounds lovely. I don't indulge my sweet tooth very often; I've found over the years the temptation isn't as great."

"Perfect," he said. "What looks good?" He scanned the dessert menu as she did the same.

"Mmm, want to share something? Maybe a little chocolate cake?"

"Sounds great," he answered, though he wanted to say that he'd get her anything she ever wanted for the rest of her life. Better to take it one thing at a time, though, and stick with chocolate cake for now.

He ordered their dessert and lightened the mood with conversation about the town and its residents. When he pushed thoughts of Eco Initiatives out of the way to focus on Zoe, he found life much more palatable. Sitting in the booth, sipping red wine and enjoying the unobstructed view of her, he actually struggled to remember why he ever thought living here was a bad idea. Their dessert arrived, and they thanked the waitress, who left before they noticed there was only one fork.

Zoe lifted her hand and craned her neck, trying to get the waitress's attention, but he sensed an opportunity and seized it. "Don't worry about it, we'll share." She turned to find him with the fork in hand, leaning across the table. With the sexiest smile he'd ever seen, she let him feed her the bite. Her eyes closed in pleasure as she tasted the chocolate icing, and he was certain he'd come undone.

He took his own bite and let the rich flavor fill his mouth. "This is probably the best thing I've ever tasted, present company excluded." He realized how cheesy that line was, and waggled his eyebrows suggestively to make a joke out of it.

She laughed, to his relief, and accepted another forkful. The little noises she made as she chewed drove him mad, the desire to climb across the table and kiss her almost impossible to resist. Before he could determine the wisdom of doing so, he quickly moved from his seat to scoot next to her in the booth. Surprise flew across her features, and she slid a few inches over so he could fit on the bench, but she didn't object. He stopped himself from feeding her chocolate sauce from his fingertips and pressed a kiss to her lips instead. The booth was dim, intimate, but they were in public, and it was still a small town, so he satisfied himself with the one chaste kiss and fed her another bite of cake.

• • •

After dessert, they stepped out into the cool evening air, the light traffic on Poplar Avenue rolling by quietly after the restaurant's more boisterous atmosphere. As their meal progressed, more patrons arrived, and by the time they were finished, the noise was such that it was easier to ignore the escalating attraction between them in favor of finishing their cake. Zoe certainly wanted more than the single kiss they shared, but she knew better than to expect privacy anywhere in town.

She lifted her shoulders a bit and gave a dramatic shiver of anticipation. "So what's next on your mysterious agenda?" As charged as that meal had been with the crackling tension between them, she wasn't sure anything would be off limits.

Adam glanced at her favorite pink, quilted satin ballet flats she chose to wear for their comfort. "I thought we'd take a little walk, so I'm glad you're wearing those." He swept his hand toward the ground. "It would be just my luck if you suddenly started wearing stilettos."

"Not a chance, at least not after I've been on my feet all day. Lead the way," she said as she tucked her hand in the crook of Adam's arm. The cotton of his shirtsleeve was soft and fine enough that she could feel his muscles contract under her touch, could feel the warmth of his skin through the fabric.

They strolled down Poplar Avenue, past all the shops she'd grown up around and the ones that had popped up as businesses changed, and walking by Adam was both incredibly exciting and surprisingly normal. It was strange to feel so comfortable with him after spending the last several years avoiding him when he visited his family. It was almost as though nothing had changed between them, as though he had never broken her heart. But he had, and in no uncertain terms. Was giving in to her feelings a foolish choice? What was she getting herself into?

Their old high school loomed ahead, and she was transported back to a simpler time. She could picture Adam so clearly, his hair longer, his body lankier. He always had a tan, which was no small feat for a teen boy living in the Pacific Northwest. His hours spent working in the tea fields ensured his perpetual glow of good health. She could picture him striding up to her locker between classes, always ready to lay a sweet kiss on her lips before hurrying off to math or history class. Now they stood on the sidewalk in front of the building, where the marquee out front proclaimed Spring Fling Tickets on Sale Now! and Congrats Lady Cardinals Volleyball Team. Adam turned to her, illuminated from behind by the street lamp, and took her hands in his.

"Annie's Arcade is where I realized I was interested in you, but this is where I fell in love with you."

"Me, too. There are a lot of memories in there."

"It's almost too good to be true," he said.

"What is?"

"To have this time together, after all we've been through. I'm amazed you've even given me a chance."

"Well, that remains to be seen. This is still a bit of a shock for me." The kisses were heavenly and the date was sublime, but she wasn't sure she could trust him with her heart. Was it foolish to enjoy their time together while they had it?

"I don't want to rush you, but I was thinking we might go make out under the bleachers." He raised his eyebrows suggestively, and she burst out laughing, covering her mouth with her hand.

She slapped his arm playfully and said, "Adam! Women my age do not make out under bleachers." At his exaggerated hangdog expression, she added with a sly grin, "We do it on top of them."

He pumped his fist, took her hand, and hurried her around back to the school's track, where a lone lamp lit the area in a soft, yellow glow. She eyed the hard metal bleachers and decided that women her age didn't make out on top of them either. The field's soft grass was inviting, though, so she continued walking past the bleachers, pulling Adam by the hand. She answered his unspoken question with a wicked grin, left her satin shoes on the dry running track, and let her bare feet sink into the soft grass, pleased to find that it wasn't damp as she'd feared. He pulled her into an embrace and looked down at her, his eyes hot with longing that reflected her own. His large hands splayed across her back, and he held her close until there was no space between them. She could feel his heartbeat under her cheek, could hear his ragged breathing in the quiet evening air. A soft breeze fluttered her skirt and she shivered, burrowing closer into his embrace.

Her eyes drifted closed as his hands moved lazily up and down her back. She snaked her arms around him, enjoying the solid feel of him. His skin's warmth seeped through his clothes, and she wondered how soft the skin under his shirt was. She tipped her face up and met his gaze, her lips parting on their own as he lowered his face to hers. He pressed a kiss to her lips, urgent and hot, and she opened her mouth under his. He deepened the kiss, and she could taste wine and chocolate, sweeter than anything she'd ever experienced. Her mind swam with emotion, lust warring with caution, desire competing with fear. It was too much to resist, and she gave herself over to the moment, pulling him down onto the soft grass where they stretched out side by side.

He pulled her close to him so that their bodies fit together perfectly, as they always had. This is what she had missed. They were like two pieces of a whole, and when they were apart, nothing was ever right. His hands wandered over her curves, setting her skin on fire with his touch. His kisses moved to her neck, down to her collarbone, across her shoulder. His hand found her breast, and he explored, gently at first as though she might stop him, and then with barely restrained enthusiasm. Her body responded to his touch, without remembering what had happened, without holding a grudge. Afraid they would eventually end up naked on the high school field, she pulled back. His eyes were half-closed, his breathing heavy, but he didn't push her to continue.

"I don't want to let you go," he whispered, his lips moving against the top of her head.

"How can you be so sure?"

Part of her wanted nothing more than to believe he was sincere, forget about the past, and get started on their happily ever after. She wasn't a naïve young girl anymore, though, and unlike her body, her brain couldn't forget.

"I don't know if I can explain it, but I've never been more certain about anything. I want to be with you, and I wish I hadn't waited so long to figure it out."

What exactly did that mean? Would she be content to date or would it take a bigger commitment? Was he proposing another long-distance relationship? This wasn't just some guy; this was Adam Whitman. There was history between them, promises and heartache, beginnings and endings. Too much to ignore, certainly too much to forget.

"But why now?"

"To be honest, I don't know. My whole life, everyone around me has tried to convince me that my place is here, that I belong at the farm. Maybe I was rebelling against expectations or something, but once I left I thought I was happier away from the family and the business. I guess I convinced myself I didn't want it, that I was happy with that new life, and didn't want to admit to myself I'd made a mistake. Instead of admitting it, I wasted time I could've spent with you."

"Assuming, of course, that I would've taken you back if you changed your mind." Her tone was gentle, but she bristled a bit at the thought that he could assume they could get back together if *he* chose.

"Of course." He kissed her forehead again, gently. "I guess I shouldn't get ahead of myself."

She sat up, pulling him with her, and kissed him chastely on the lips. "This is nice, you and me, but I feel like I should make you work harder," she teased, lightening the tone after the heavy turn the conversation had taken. "I'm not like the other girls in this town. I don't just fall for any guy with the Whitman name."

He smiled briefly but then turned serious as he cupped her face in his hands and looked into her eyes. "It's been a long time coming, but I know what I want. I'm sure that I want you; I want us. I'm willing to do whatever it takes to show you. I don't know how it will work, but I know we can figure something out."

He stood and helped her to her feet before taking her hand and leading her to the track where her shoes were waiting. "I want you to think about this, really think about it. I can't change the past, but I can try to make you happy now. Let me take you home. We can talk about it again tomorrow night."

He waited while she slid her feet into her shoes then took her hand and walked with her across the school property until they were back on the sidewalk. Part of her wanted to ditch her misgivings and just make out with him. It would be so nice to just give into the desire swirling around them, to go for it and pretend he wouldn't be gone again by the end of the week. It had been too long for her, and he had only gotten better with age, but there was so much history. After all they'd been through, they could never just date. This wouldn't be a fling; this could be the real thing if she allowed him back into her life. How could she trust him with her heart again?

"So, what happened at your dad's office today?"

His hand tightened around hers, and his profile hardened in the soft glow of the street lights. "Somebody," he said with clenched teeth, "called Immigration and reported that we have undocumented workers at the farm. Dad says that it happens sometimes, that it's nothing to worry about since his operations are all above-board."

"But still, it's got to be stressful. You should have told me earlier." With so many employees working on the farm, keeping records must be a gargantuan task.

"I was too angry, didn't want to spoil our evening."

"You don't have to protect me from bad news, you know." Things shifted between them, became more real as she realized that she wanted to know what happened on the farm, that she worried about the family. "I'm not just here for the chocolate cake. What happened? Did they find something?" Richard Whitman was a solid citizen, not one to skirt the law. Still, mistakes could be made with so many employees to account for.

"No, there was nothing to find. If they just came to the office and ended up leaving without any trouble, it would have been bad enough. They basically asked for a bribe to make it all go away, said that they could make things very easy or really difficult for the farm."

"Are you serious?"

"Yeah. I kind of lost my temper at that point, and actually shoved one of them out the door when he didn't move fast enough."

"Oh my gosh. What did your dad say?"

He smiled. "That he was glad to see I care about the farm. That scumbag had it coming, but I can't lose control like that. It's just asking for a lawsuit, although he also said that the company has an excellent attorney."

"It's probably not a bad idea to take control of the situation."

"What do you mean?"

"I mean you should probably report those guys. If they're bold enough to shake down Richard Whitman, I can only imagine what they're doing to smaller farms in the county. When it comes down to it, you shoving one of them out the door is nothing compared to what they're doing."

"You're right. They are probably extorting thousands from people too scared to stand up to them."

"Call the Immigration office first thing in the morning and get ahead of this. You're probably the first one to stand up to them if they were bold enough to try it at Emerald Tea Farm."

Adam smiled down at her and took her hands in his. "I'm glad I talked to you about it. We make a good team."

Chapter Eight

Adam walked into the main office, his mind on how he would establish his place at the company once he took his place at its helm. Emerald Springs was pulling him in—not to mention Zoe—but his life in L.A. was one he'd built by himself, not on the strength of the Whitman name, and he couldn't let it go without serious consideration. At Eco Initiatives, he was on his way to becoming someone who made people sit up and take notice. He'd always wanted to live a life less ordinary, to make a difference, to be somebody. He could do that in L.A., or he could do that in Emerald Springs.

Chatter and a heavenly aroma pulled him into the employee kitchen on his way to his dad's office. A group crowded around a table, riveted by the baby pictures one of them was showing off. His arrival didn't cause so much as a pause in their conversation, but if he left his job and took his place here, everyone would know who he was, and he'd have the recognition he craved, in addition to the power he'd be giving up if he left his job in L.A. to return. The promotion at Eco Initiatives was big, but it wasn't CEO of a national brand. Taking over his father's position would be important work, satisfying work, and he could be happy here.

He grabbed a cup and poured himself a sample of the brand's newest blend, Berry Dairy, a black tea with strong strawberry and vanilla notes. Funny how since coming back to Washington, he'd rediscovered his enthusiasm for the family product—and suddenly the time to brew it was there. Every blend was unique and delicious, obviously perfected before being offered to the public. Emerald Tea Farm was a brand he was going to be proud to represent, and more and more it was becoming clear this was where he belonged. Seeing how much the farm and company itself had grown was enough to get his wheels turning, but the emotional connection he felt during the confrontation with the Immigration officials surprised him more than anything. He'd been so certain that he didn't care about the family legacy, didn't see the company as an extension of his heritage. Fiercely defending it gave him that surge of adrenaline he'd thought he would miss if he took the position here. The connection between him and the company was stronger, more important than he thought.

If only he hadn't looked at the generous compensation package Eco Initiative's partners were willing to offer him. Corner office, forty percent salary increase, Lakers seasons tickets, plus the authority and visibility he'd been striving for. If only the increased responsibility and excitement of his potential new post, and the certainty that it would put him in a position to negotiate and implement his own programs instead of carrying out the dreams of others weren't calling to him, drawing him away from the farm.

He sipped his tea and nodded to the ladies as he left them in the kitchen and ambled down the hallway to meet his father. If this were Eco Initiatives, Adam would be in the thick of it, drinking coffee and adjusting his bluetooth phone headset, ready to brainstorm with some of the most brilliant minds in environmental science, to negotiate deals, and implement programs that would bring major changes to huge corporations. Nobody would blink an eye when he suggested initiatives that changed companies' cultures, even when they cost millions. His initiatives would bring about real change, real environmental benefits. He'd never found anything that could replace the rush of seeing an idea come to fruition, of creating solutions to problems. Would he be able to find that here?

He laughed to himself, imagining what employees here would think if they saw him storming through the offices wearing a headset, barking orders to a subordinate. They'd likely laugh him right out of the building. It was amazing how different the pace at Emerald Tea Farm seemed; they were certainly accomplishing the same amount of work, just without the high blood pressure and heartburn.

His dad was already behind his desk, fingers tapping on his keyboard, phone balanced between his ear and shoulder when Adam greeted him. He held up a finger and gestured for him to take a seat while he finished his call. He sat in one of a pair of rich brown leather captain's chairs, absorbing the welcoming but professional space that perfectly reflected his father's personality. The beige walls were calming without being boring white, while beautifully framed photographs of the farm and artistic shots of Emerald Eats and Emerald Paradise, the family resort, lined the walls. Dad had likely purchased them from a local photographer and had them framed, as nothing was more important to Richard Whitman than his family and their enterprises. His sturdy bookshelves housed binders, books, and smaller framed photographs of the family. Everybody was represented, even Zoe and Patty, on those shelves. His dad spent more time at work than he did at home most days; it made sense that his office reflected his true loves.

He ended his call and turned to Adam with an easy smile. "Good morning," he said, taking a deep sniff. "That smells like Berry Dairy; what do you think?"

"It's delicious. It might be my new favorite."

"I'm pretty pleased with that one. I'm thinking of talking with Ashley about putting it together in a bundle with Cherry Berry Spice so it'll catch on faster. I'd like to look at different ways we can capitalize on some of the blends made from the fruits we grow on site."

"I'm impressed. Growing up, I never realized how much went into all this; I just thought you were making tea."

"I think there are still things around here that will surprise you."

"Oh, I know there are. So, I was thinking more about our little run-in with the Immigration guys yesterday."

"Yeah?"

"Yeah. Zoe and I talked about it last night, and she suggested that I report them, and I think she was right. She reasoned that if they were bold enough to come in here and try to extort money from you, then chances were good that they were running roughshod over the smaller farms in the area."

His father leaned forward on his elbows, his eyes serious. "Good point. Did you call?"

"Not yet. I didn't want to plow ahead with it if you had other ideas. You're still CEO, after all."

"I think you and Zoe are right. We need to report them. She's a sharp one."

"She is." Adam hadn't ever given her the respect she deserved, hadn't seen her as the savvy, competent woman that she'd become. "So, you want to do the honors, or should I?"

"I'll have Arlene find the number, and I'd love for you to do it, unless you've decided for sure that you're not interested in becoming CEO. Otherwise, this is one of those things that will establish the kind of leader you're going to be."

"I'll do it." Adam didn't know if he was agreeing to the phone call or the position, but he wasn't saying no to either. The satisfied look on his father's face told him he was knitting himself further into the fiber of Emerald Tea Farm, whether he was ready or not.

"Arlene?" His father spoke into the intercom on his desk. "Could you connect us to the Immigration office?" His dad opened a drawer and pulled out one of the company's signature emerald green folders and passed it across the desk. "Have a look while we wait."

"What is it?" He took the file and scanned the text.

"They are plans, really, nothing more yet. I thought it might be a good time to make a formal offer on some of Split Acres's land that abuts our property rather than hope Joe responds to hints. The Berry Dairy is the first blend to make good use of our strawberries, and it's already got a lot of buzz. I'd like to expand on that, but I'll need more space for crops. We could add more fruits if we had more room."

"I thought they weren't organic over there. How would you even use their land?" Adam had a lot to learn about the business, but he knew the standards that regulated organic farming were strict. And Joe hadn't concerned himself with them in many years.

"We have the buffer between our two properties to comply with regulations, so I was hoping to move the line and use our buffer, which is chemical-free. The land we'd buy from them would start the new buffer."

"Well that makes sense, but when was the last time you even talked to Joe?" Their former business partner was notoriously stubborn.

"It's been a while, that's true, but business is business. Surely if they need the money and we need the space, we can come to a mutually advantageous agreement. If Joe isn't interested, then I'm sure Colleen will try to talk some sense into him."

Adam nodded. "Yeah, I hadn't considered that. She'd probably see the wisdom in it immediately even if he wants to refuse."

"That's what I'm counting on, actually. I was thinking we could go out there and meet with her before he gets a chance to shoot us down."

"That's smart."

"So you have time for a little field trip?"

"Of course. I would love to get up close and personal with you," Adam teased. It was no small thing that making a big deal before he even officially signed on would start off his tenure as CEO on the right foot.

"When you accept my offer to take over the farm, we'll spend so much time together that by the time you're ready to take the wheel solo, we'll be good and sick of each other," his dad said with a laugh. "I'm glad you're here for this, though. You and Colleen have always gotten along—she might be more likely to listen to you, especially if she gets the impression you're the one she's going to be dealing with in the future. We don't have to say you haven't actually made plans to take over. I don't know how much her dad's opinion of me has carried over, so she could say no just because I'm there."

"I can't remember the last time I saw Colleen, but we've always been friendly ... well, except for that time she punched me in the nose when we were kids."

"Well, Joe still blames me for everything. She may feel the same way, or she may consider it his fight; I don't know. I've been interested in pursuing this for a while, but I haven't been able to get a good read on how it'll be received so I know how to best approach the deal."

"Then this is perfect timing. I'd love to get in on a new deal from the beginning." Having a hand in brokering the deal and expanding the company would be perfect to kick off his new position.

"Read over what I've got, and we can firm up our game plan before we head over there." Adam nodded and studied the plan. This could be a great way to see how he'd like taking control of the business—if it could compare to the million dollar projects he'd be missing if he left Eco Initiatives. Brokering a deal right off the bat would surely show his father that he was making a wise decision, and the plan outlined in the papers looked easy enough to sell. He just hoped Colleen would be the first one they saw at Split Acres. Joe Sanders would be a much harder sell.

"Mr. Whitman?" the assistant's voice came through the intercom. "I have Immigration on line one."

"Thank you, Arlene," his father picked up the receiver and pressed a button on the phone before handing it to Adam.

"Hello?" Adam tensed, his blood boiling as he thought of the agents' outrageous behavior. "This is Adam Whitman, calling on behalf of Emerald Tea Farm in reference to our investigation."

"Good morning, Mr. Whitman." He heard a keyboard clacking on the other end of the line. "I'll pull up your case and will be able to direct you to the correct office. One moment, please." The female voice was pleasant, efficient. "Hmm. That's odd. I don't have a case number for you. Let me transfer you to Investigations; maybe they can help you. One moment please."

With a click, "hold" music came through the line, and Adam waited for the next person to answer. He covered the mouthpiece with his hand and addressed his dad. "The lady couldn't find us in the system. I'm being transferred to Investigations."

"Investigations," a male voice answered this time, abrupt and jarring.

"Hello, this is Adam Whitman, calling on behalf of Emerald Tea Farm. Two investigators responded to an anonymous tip regarding the legal status of our seasonal workforce, and I'd like to lodge a complaint regarding their behavior."

"What happened?" A heavy sigh followed the man's question. Adam figured that nobody who called the Immigration office was happy.

"They were afforded free access to our employment records, and we accommodated their investigation without hesitation. After they examined the files, they attempted to extort money from us in order for them to find in our favor. We have never had trouble with your office in the past, and I was shocked that these two would be so brazen in their attempt to bribe us."

"Mr. Whitman, I'm sorry, but I don't have a complaint against Emerald Tea Farm. I've pulled up all the information we have on you, and we haven't had an agent visit your premises for years."

Adam's stomach dropped. "What are you saying?"

"I'm saying whoever visited you yesterday was not from our office, sir."

"Thank you." Adam handed the phone to his dad and slumped in the chair as he replaced it in the cradle. "They weren't from Immigration, Dad."

"We were set up." His father's mouth set in a grim line.

"But by whom?"

His father shrugged. "I don't know. Could be somebody just trying to see how much they could squeeze out of us, or someone looking for information."

"It's a good day to head over to Split Acres, then, so we can watch how Joe Sanders reacts. If he seems suspicious, we might have our answer."

"I'll report it to the sheriff's office nonetheless. They should open an investigation, whether this is an isolated incident or someone targeting farms in the county. We'll keep our eyes and ears open, but this is a criminal matter, not something we can handle by confronting Joe or anything." His dad turned his computer monitor off and rose, ready to visit Split Acres.

• • •

Adam sat in the passenger seat of his father's pickup truck and rolled down the side window, determined to imprint the experience on his mind, to remember why he wanted to come back when he started to second guess himself. They rolled past fields of tea and he promised himself he wouldn't get caught up in the craziness when he went back to his office. He'd remember what he loved about this place, he'd keep Zoe in the front of his mind, and he would make his choice with a clear head. It didn't matter what exciting new projects could be starting at Eco Initiatives, what crises might need his expertise. He could be happy at the head of Emerald Tea Farm, and he would look forward, not back. He was going to come back to Emerald Springs, and he was going to make Zoe his wife, something he couldn't live here without. It was all coming together.

They pulled into the driveway at Split Acres and his father turned to him. "You ready to do this?"

"As ready as I'll ever be. It's a good idea, Dad. Surely Joe can put aside the past to make a business deal."

His father laughed, short and hard. "You'd be surprised. That man can hold a grudge like nobody's business. You have no idea how many times I've extended the olive branch, tried to at least be civil neighbors. He's not interested."

"Then I guess we have our work cut out for us. Let's just hope we run into Colleen first."

He opened the door and hopped out of the truck, closing the door with more enthusiasm than was necessary. As he stood in the driveway, he stretched a bit and surveyed the site. The atmosphere at Split Acres was decidedly less industrious than down the road at Emerald Tea Farm. A handful of bedraggled employees did the work more appropriate for a workforce twice their size; the air was heavier, more depressing to him. They were standing literally right down the road from the farm thriving with beautiful crops and busy workers, but Split Acres was like a whole different world. He followed his father up the walkway to a utilitarian office building and held the door open for him. At least the air inside was cool and welcoming, despite the worn industrial gray carpet, outdated motel art hanging on the walls, and the tired-looking secretary sitting at a desk.

They approached the woman and waited for her to end her phone call. She looked up and gave them a bored stare until his dad spoke up. "Is Joe Sanders available?"

"And you are?" If she started chomping bubble gum, Adam wouldn't be surprised.

"Richard and Adam Whitman," he responded.

The bottled blonde raised her eyebrows. "Whitman? Emerald Tea Whitman?"

"Yes ma'am, the very same," Adam replied in a voice he hoped was disarming.

"One moment, please. I'll see if he's available." The woman turned her chair to a bookcase behind her and grabbed a walkie-talkie off its charger. "Colleen?"

A disembodied voice answered, "Go."

"Two gentlemen are here to see your father in the front office. Richard and Adam Whitman. Is he on site today?"

"I'll be right there," the little voice replied.

"You gentleman can have a seat; Colleen will be right in." The woman indicated a couple of worn, gray chairs that looked like they'd were in service before Joe went his separate way and then turned her attention to her computer screen. He could just make out the corner of her solitaire game.

The office was quiet, the only sound the receptionist's mouse clicks as the minutes stretched between them. Tension rolled off his father so thick Adam could almost feel it. It was probably difficult for him to face his old friend and partner, and Colleen wasn't that much different. He rarely spoke about the business he and Joe Sanders shared, much less the conflict that led to their split, but seeing Split Acres suffer must have made him feel guilty, though he had no part in Joe's success or failure and hadn't for ages.

The office door opened, bringing with it sunshine and Colleen Sanders. They were on their feet in an instant and walking toward her. To Adam's eyes, she had barely aged since high school. She was still tan and lean, still wore her hair in the same messy bun—hell, her flannel shirt was probably one she had in high school. It was old and faded from years of wear, a sharp contrast to the bright pink rubber rain boots covered in a whimsical pinwheel design. Beads of sweat glistened on her forehead, and she ran the back of her hand across her face. She was pretty, beautiful even, but she didn't look happy to see them. He tossed aside thoughts of reminiscing about high school to soften her reaction to them.

"Mr. Whitman, Adam, what can I do for you?" she asked without preamble.

"Hey Colleen," he said easily, flashing the smile most girls couldn't resist.

"Hey," she replied, clearly unaffected.

"We were hoping to see your dad. Is he around?"

"Nope. He's out of town." She was closed off, clearly not interested in a chatty reunion.

"Okay, that's fine. I'm happy to talk with you about it, since you basically run the place. We have a proposal for you, a business proposition, and hoped you had a minute to talk about it," his father took over. "Do you have an office or somewhere we can discuss it with you?"

"Right here's fine; I've got a lot of work to do. What is it you want to ask me?" She wasn't being outright hostile, but Colleen made it clear that she wasn't interested in a long visit.

"All right. It's all spelled out here in the proposal, and I will leave it with you to go over in detail later, maybe with your dad. Basically, we're interested in leasing or purchasing a piece of Split Acres. Of course the size is negotiable based on what you can spare and what you're interested in letting go. We need more land, and a lot of the area that abuts our property would be perfect," his father explained.

He held out the file folder for her, but she crossed her arms. "That's okay. I don't think we're interested in selling."

"We would also consider a fixed-term lease. We could try it out and revisit it at a mutually agreeable time," Adam offered, his easy smile still doing nothing to crack her icy exterior.

"No, thank you." Her voice was sharp, brooking no further discussion.

The receptionist's head snapped up, her eyes comically wide, before she bustled out of the office. The atmosphere crackled with tension, and Adam couldn't figure out where they had gone wrong with Colleen. She was determined to dismiss anything they had to say, and she didn't care how rudely she was doing it.

He stepped a foot closer to her and laid a light hand on her shoulder. To his chagrin, she shrugged it off and gave him an indecipherable look. "Let me just leave this with you," he said as he took the folder from his father and placed it on the desk. "We'll be in touch. We have obviously come by at a bad time."

"Thanks for your time," his father echoed.

They walked quickly back to the truck without a word. Once they were back on the road, they turned to one another with mutually dumbfounded expressions.

"What the hell was that all about?"

"I thought that blonde lady was going to give herself whiplash." Adam felt the tension dissipate a bit now that they were out of the office, and he had to laugh. "You know, I thought things might be a little awkward in there, but I never would've guessed Colleen would act like that. We were never best friends or anything, but we always got along fine before; I don't know what that was all about."

"It looks like we'll have to figure something else out. I doubt that proposal is anywhere but in the old circular file right now." His dad took his eyes off the road long enough to flick a look toward him. "Does it seem strange that she was so fast to say no? It's almost like she knew why we were there and didn't want any part of it."

He shrugged. "I guess it was a little weird. We didn't talk about it to anyone else before going over there, though, so how would she have known?"

"You know, I haven't come out and shared my plan with Joe, but I'll bet someone leaked it. I've been asking around, trying to get information from the other guys, and there's a chance somebody started talking. You know how those old farmers love their gossip. It also makes me wonder if maybe we shouldn't keep an eye on Marlon, with him showing up so much lately and working for Joe." Richard scraped a hand over his face and exhaled. "We've seen a little too much of him lately, and it might not be coincidence. I never thought Joe was the scheming type, but he might surprise us."

"People change," Adam said with a shrug. "Colleen was the real surprise though. Did you get a look at her boots?"

"With the pinwheels?"

"Yeah, you know she's tough if she can stare us down wearing pink boots covered in pinwheels." He laughed and turned back to watch the scenery roll by out his window.

"True." His dad nodded his head once and parked the truck at the farm.

Adam looked at his watch and frowned. "I'm running late now."

"You got big plans this evening?" he asked, lightening the mood.

"I'm going to take Zoe out again, but maybe I should postpone. We need to figure out what we're going to do about those Immigration scumbags." Just anticipating seeing her again gave him a warm jolt of excitement despite himself.

"I'll go in and make sure nothing's been tampered with, and we can discuss this again tomorrow. I don't want you to let Zoe down; I'm sure she'd be disappointed if you cancel your date. How are things going with her?"

"It's going all right. She's really cautious about me, but at least she hasn't told me to take a hike yet," Adam joked. "I'm still surprised about that, to tell you the truth."

His dad gave him a sober look. "Second chances are rare. Take good care of yours."

"I will. I know if I screw it up again, she'll be done with me."

"No pressure though," his dad said with a short laugh and a quick pat on his shoulder. "Have a good time tonight."

•••

Spruce Street was lined with cars, with people shuffling in and out of the downtown shops, and Adam parked several stores away from Zoe's bakery. Gray skies and heavy clouds overhead threatened rain, but he hummed as he made his way to her shop, a spring in his step. He jangled his keys in his hand and checked out his reflection in the windows that he passed. With any luck, she would like what she saw. Perhaps another kiss would soften her up and his words would do the rest; before long, she'd see that he was serious about them. He wouldn't even consider the possibility that she'd refuse him. At this point, his entire decision whether to stay in Emerald Springs or go back to L.A. depended on having her back in his life. He was on his way to falling in love with the farm, could already see that he was more invested in it than he'd thought, but he wanted the whole package. He wouldn't be able to rub elbows with her at the farm or family dinners if they weren't a couple, wouldn't want to live here if she were just a family friend. He couldn't go back to being just friends; he wouldn't.

Adam stopped on the sidewalk, his stomach flipping over. Marlon was climbing down from a rundown, rust brown pickup truck, his eyes trained on the bakery. Few things would derail his romantic plans for the evening, like Zoe having to deal with another incident with her father. He hurried to intercept him on the sidewalk before the man could walk in front of the bakery's windows.

"Hey, Marlon," he began, cautious but trying to appear casual. "What's going on?"

Marlon was obviously surprised to see him and eyed him a bit suspiciously. "Not much, just getting off work. I'm meeting a few buddies at The Rusty Tap for some beers."

"Is that right? That sounds like fun." Adam rocked back on his heels and looked down at him. "It kind of seems like you are heading for Zoe's place."

"What are you, a cop? So what if I am going to see my daughter?"

Adam laughed and put his hands up defensively. "I wasn't accusing you of anything, just making an observation. I'm actually heading over there myself. Can I help you with something?"

"What's that supposed to mean?" Marlon narrowed his eyes, and if Adam hadn't been so intent on making the evening perfect, it would have been comical.

The men stopped in front of the bakery, right on the edge of the window. Adam couldn't see Zoe inside, but if she walked by she would surely see them. "Look, no offense or disrespect intended, but were you going in to borrow money from Zoe? Because, listen, I'd like to help." He pulled his wallet out of his back pocket and flipped it open with his thumb.

Marlon pushed the wallet away. "I don't need your money, man."

Zoe was at the door, watching, but he couldn't tell by her expression what she was thinking. How much of the exchange had she witnessed? She opened the door and poked her head out. "What's going on out here?"

"I was just coming to see you, sweetheart." Marlon moved away from Adam and headed to the door.

She stepped out onto the sidewalk, her blue eyes huge with concern. "Are you feeling all right? You don't look so good."

Marlon swayed a bit, and Adam noticed that he looked a little green. Zoe put the back of her hand on his forehead and furrowed her brow. "You're clammy but burning up. You should be home in bed."

"Nah, I'm fine. I was heading down to The Rusty Tap to see if anyone was playing pool tonight when Adam stopped me." He jerked his thumb toward Adam.

"I think Zoe's right. You look like you could use some rest. Where's your car?"

Marlon's shoulders slumped. "It's down the street, but I'm low on gas."

Zoe gently laid her hand on her father's shoulder. "Let me grab my purse, Dad, and we'll take you home. You want something to eat?"

He looked like he wanted to refuse for a moment before nodding. "Sure, honey. A little something would probably be good."

"Hold on a second. I'll be right back." Zoe disappeared into the bakery.

Left alone with Marlon, Adam saw what had Zoe so concerned. His complexion was waxy, and sweat beaded his forehead. He was so accustomed to seeing Marlon as a nuisance, as someone to be quickly dispatched, that he'd ignored the signs that he might need help. "Do you need a doctor?"

"Nah, I'm okay. Don't tell Zoe, but, uh, I'm not sick. I'm trying to quit drinking, and it's kicking my ass."

"I think Zoe would think that's great. Why don't you want her know?"

"It's, uh, not exactly my first time. Better to wait and see how it goes before I get her hopes up."

"Ah, I see. Well then, good luck. If you want our help, just ask."

Zoe returned with a bag of food and a box of green tea bags. "All right, let's get you home and into bed."

"I'll drive." Adam offered and was rewarded with Zoe's grateful look.

They helped Marlon into the backseat of Adam's rental car and drove the short distance to his house in Meyerville in silence. Adam waited in the car, giving them some privacy as Zoe helped Marlon into his house. She returned and slipped into the passenger's seat without a word.

"Got him settled in?" Adam kept his tone light, not wanting to embarrass her.

"Yep." She folded her hands in her lap and turned away from him as he pulled out of the driveway. "Thanks." Her voice was almost a whisper.

Adam put his hand on her thigh as he navigated through the neighborhood, past a house with a couch on the porch. "Of course. I'm glad we could help him get home safely. You're a good daughter."

"Yeah, well, he needs me."

"I know, and he's lucky to have you." It was easy to think of Marlon as an unrepentant drunk, someone who caused all the trouble that plagued him, but seeing him so weak and clearly in need softened Adam. No wonder Zoe was so conflicted when it came to choosing L.A. or Emerald Springs.

Cars lined Spruce Street, and Adam had to park half a dozen stores away from Everything Nice. As he unbuckled his seatbelt, Adam angled his body to face Zoe. "You did a good thing, taking care of your dad. Let's go close up the shop so I can take you out for a nice dinner. You deserve it."

She squared her shoulders and took a deep breath. "Thanks. For everything."

Adam grinned and hurried around to the passenger door, eager to get her mind off Marlon and on to more pleasant things. A fat raindrop landed on his face, and he noticed the darkened sky over downtown Emerald Springs. The people milling around outside started moving faster, shuffling between destinations as more rain began to fall. He opened her door and held out his hand to help her out of the car. Rain began to fall in earnest as they ducked their heads and hurried towards Everything Nice, hand in hand. Adam pulled a soaked Zoe under the awning at her bakery's door and wrapped his arms around her.

"I don't want to get your floor all wet."

"I know, we're soaked to the bone. Courtney can lock up, and I'll check everything out in the morning." He could feel the vibrations from her voice against his chest. She rapped on the door to get her assistant's attention and motioned that she should lock up. Courtney nodded, and Zoe turned her attention back to Adam.

He kissed the top of her head and inhaled deeply, enjoying the sweet smell of vanilla and sugar. "So I guess you're all mine now."

She inched closer, snuggling in and closing the small space between them, and his breath caught in his throat. He ran a hand down the back of her head, smoothing her damp hair with his touch, and tilted her face up to meet his. He dropped a soft kiss onto her lips and felt her relax in his arms. Her lips were warm and sweet, like she had licked the frosting off of a spatula earlier. He coaxed her lips open and deepened the kiss, enjoying the exotic but familiar feeling of her mouth. She returned his kiss with growing enthusiasm, gripping him tighter. She shivered against him and he pulled back, his eyes taking in her body beneath the clinging wet fabric of her clothes. A grin spread across her face, and his body responded.

She took his hand in hers, rubbing his skin with her thumb, and bit her bottom lip. She looked up at him with blue eyes hazy with desire. "I guess we'll need to get out of these wet clothes before we go on our date."

"I guess so." His throat was thick and it was hard to breathe. She was simply beautiful, standing on the sidewalk, soaked to the bone, in the late afternoon's lazy sunlight.

"Come on. Let me change clothes, and we'll figure something out for you." She pulled his hand, leading him toward the stairs to her apartment.

He followed , certain he couldn't resist her if he wanted to. Not that he wanted to. She climbed the stairs to her apartment with him close behind, so close he could feel her body's warmth but not so close that he couldn't enjoy the view. He kept his hands on the rail as they ascended the steps, careful not to take liberties with her tempting backside. She unlocked her door and looked back at him, a knowing smile crossing her lips. He followed her inside where the cool air gave his rain-soaked body a chill.

"Give me just a second." She pulled a couple of fluffy towels from her linen closet and handed him the stack with an apologetic look. "I'm going to change, and then I guess we should run by your dad's place to get you into some dry clothes." She disappeared into her room, leaving him in the middle of the living room holding the towels, unsure how that would help with the soaked clothes.

He unfolded one and rubbed it over his hair and face, trying to think of something, anything, other than a naked Zoe a few yards away from him, nothing but a door separating them. What would she do if he knocked? She had been so receptive to him this afternoon, something he couldn't take for granted after the heavy conversation that ended their last date. He didn't want to push his luck, not yet at least. She knew he was interested, and she could steer the date whichever way she liked. He would keep his hands to himself if that's what she wanted. If she wanted more, then of course he'd be happy to oblige. She stepped out of her bedroom, and his body responded to the sight of her before his brain could form a coherent thought. She was wearing the smallest, softest-looking pink shorts he'd ever seen and a matching tank top. No bra. Her hair hung in damp waves around her shoulders, and her face was clean, scrubbed of makeup. She wasn't dressed to leave the apartment, and he had never seen her look more beautiful.

She took another step closer and trained her eyes on her feet for a moment that stretched out between them before looking up again. He swallowed against the lump forming in his throat when she finally spoke. "Maybe we can just stay here."

"Okay," he managed to whisper. He'd stay in cold, wet clothes, as long as he could be here with her.

Zoe kept her eyes on his chest as she pulled his shirt from the waistband of his pants and slowly undid each button. He struggled to keep his breathing normal, certain his heart would pound out of his chest if she made eye contact. She pushed his wet shirt over his shoulders and dropped it in a heap on the floor. With her hands on his skin, he lost his last shred of restraint. He pulled her against his hips and claimed her mouth in a kiss that left no question as to his intentions. She returned his kiss with an intensity that matched his own as she pressed her body against his, her breasts crushed against his chest. He held her face in his hands, enjoying her soft skin and silky hair still damp from the rain. She pushed him back until he dropped onto the couch. She stood before him for a moment, and his senses blurred with lust, his body hardening at the sight of her.

She gave him a devilish smile and straddled his lap, where their bodies matched perfectly. She wrapped her arms around him and lowered her head until their lips touched again, pressing a soft kiss on his lips before trailing kisses across his cheek. She made her way to his ear, where she nibbled and laughed softly as he sighed, her breath hot against his skin. Her lips laid a hot path down his neck, and he gripped her tighter, his hands splaying against her back and relishing the feel of her warm skin under the thin fabric of her tiny shirt. She rocked against him, bringing him right to the edge, and then slowed her pace to move her lips back to rest on his. His eyes closed as he reveled in the sensations she awoke in him. She treated him to another deep, slow kiss, sweet and unrestrained. Their tongues tangled together until he was certain he would strain right out of his pants.

She smiled against his lips and walked her fingertips down to his waistband, scooting back on his lap enough to give herself room to reach him. She unbuckled his belt and pulled it out of the loops with an incredibly sexy little laugh before tossing it onto the floor. He watched her with hooded eyes, this woman both so familiar to him and such a mystery. His senses were overloaded with her, with the feel of her soft skin, the scent of vanilla wafting over him when she moved. Even the air was charged with desire and an urgency Adam had never felt before. Not with Zoe when they were young, and definitely not with any other woman since.

She ran her fingers through his hair and leaned close to whisper in his ear. "Take me to my bed."

Adam didn't need any further encouragement. He scooped her up and carried her into her bedroom. He heard her throaty, sexy laugh, and he knew he would never be the same again.

Chapter Nine

Adam dropped her gently on her bed and stood at the foot, openly raking his gaze up and down her body, and Zoe was sure she would burst with need. She lay propped up on her elbows and gave him her most alluring look.

"Lose the pants and come here," she said as she beckoned him with a hooked finger.

He gave her the sexiest smile she'd ever seen and dropped his pants, leaving them in a heap on the floor. He lowered himself onto her bed until he was hovering just inches above her, supported on his arms. He pushed her legs apart with his knees and settled in between her thighs, nestling himself snugly against her. She could feel his erection straining against the fabric of his boxers through the thin fabric of her shorts and swiveled her hips up to meet him. She had never felt so desperate for a man's touch, so wild with passion for someone—not even Adam himself. When they were together before, things had never been like this. He groaned and swooped down to capture her mouth in a desperate kiss. Their tongues moved across one another in a heated dance, wild in their need. One hand found her breast and he stroked her over the fabric of her top until she broke the kiss and threw her head back in abandon.

He pulled her up until she was sitting and yanked her shirt over her head, tossing it behind him onto the floor with his pants. He kissed her again, and her sounds of pleasure urged him to deepen the kiss. He breathed across her neck, giving her goose bumps all the way down to her toes.

He whispered in her ear, his voice raspy with need, "God, you're so beautiful, Zoe." The sound of her name on his lips sent a frisson of pleasure through her. "I've never wanted anyone but you." His lips on hers stopped any response, and before she could consider what his words meant, her head was fuzzy with desire again.

She clutched his shoulders and shuddered with anticipation as he laid her down onto her back and lowered his lips to her collarbone. He trailed a line of soft, teasing kisses across her skin before moving down. He cupped her breasts in his hands and gently flicked his thumbs over her nipples before lowering his mouth to one and pulling it in. His tongue rolled around, sending a shock of pleasure right to her core. She thrust her fingers through his silky, dark hair and held his head in place, encouraging him. Her hips bucked up to meet his and he smiled against her skin before moving to the other breast to lavish the same treatment on it. She bit her lip and stifled a moan, not certain she could take much more.

As though reading her signals, he moved his attention to her neck, kissing her sensitive skin while his hand continued to cup her breast. He stroked her with his thumb until she thought she would burst. His finger trailed down her body, over the planes of her stomach, until he reached the apex of her thighs.

"I've wanted this, since the moment I first saw you the other day," he said.

"Me, too," she admitted, breathless.

His lips pressed against hers, first gently and then with rising urgency. His fingers caressed her between her legs, exploring softly before sliding first one finger and then another inside. She writhed under him at his touch, positive she would come apart if he didn't take her soon. She stroked his hardened length over his boxers before pushing them over his hips and down his legs. He shifted until he could kick them off, rocked back on his knees, and pulled her shorts off in one smooth motion. He raked his eyes over her body, clearly enjoying the sight, and lowered his head to between her thighs. She sucked in a breath as his lips found her, licking languorous strokes that drove her mad. When she couldn't take any more, he finally moved up to kiss her thighs, her stomach, her hips. She flipped over and stretched until she could reach her nightstand drawer.

"Give me one second," she whispered.

She rummaged around blindly until her fingers found a foil packet, and she returned to her spot on the bed, centered under his body. She wiggled the packet and ripped it open playfully. He snapped it out of her hand with a rakish grin and sheathed himself. Rocking back on his heels again, his desire for her clearly evident, he was gorgeous. From his achingly beautiful and familiar face to the hard planes of his body, there was nobody she'd ever wanted more.

She closed her eyes and inhaled his familiar and distinctly masculine scent as he hovered over her, his skin radiating warmth. He lowered his lips to her neck and kissed her, softly and sweetly, as he stroked her skin with a feather-light touch. She shivered against him and swiveled her hips up to meet him, feeling the hard evidence of his desire for her. He claimed her lips in a kiss that answered the questions she hadn't asked as he entered her. She moaned into his mouth at the sensation, joined with the man a part of her would always love, and he began to move inside her. He was gentle, exploring, until her body responded with growing intensity. His rhythm matched hers, and they moved in harmony until she felt the exquisite sensations build to an incredible height within her. She clutched his back, reveling in the feeling of soft skin covering powerful muscles, as her climax crashed through her. He kissed her as her mind cleared and she returned to the moment. Her legs wrapped around his back and pulled him close as his rhythm increased and she held his face in her hands, locking eyes with him as he reached his own climax.

Exhausted, he collapsed on top of her, covering her body with his in delicious warmth and weight before rolling to her side. She curled her body to mold against his, and his fingers traced a lazy trail over the curves of her leg and hip, up over her ribs and across her shoulder. He cupped her face and looked into her eyes before bringing her lips to his. He kissed her softly, somehow managing to impart a world of emotion in the contact.

"That was amazing," he said. "Even better than I hoped."

"You hoped? Was this on your agenda for tonight?" She giggled and snuggled into his embrace.

"Hey, a guy can dream. I was planning on taking you to the old house, thinking it might remind you of the first time we were together. I thought the memories might win you over." He pushed the hair away from her face.

"Were you hoping to take me upstairs so you could seduce me in your old twin bed, just like the first time?" Flashes of their sweet, fumbling encounter drifted through her mind. Losing her virginity to Adam was something she had never regretted, and now that he was back in her life, it was that much sweeter.

He laughed. "I think my old room is an office or a storage room now. It would have to be in my parents' old bedroom, which now that I say it out loud doesn't sound like a great idea."

"You did okay with that house the first time around. I'd say it was a pretty good bet you could do it again."

"When I planned tonight's date, it seemed more sophisticated. I'm glad it worked out like this, though. My intentions couldn't hold a candle to this."

"Just don't get the idea I'm some cheap date. You can't expect that every time you come to pick me up, we'll get soaked with rain and cancel the date."

He snapped his fingers. "Damn. That was going to be my strategy." He kissed her before pulling her closer, wrapping his arms around her.

"You'll have to do better than that. We've got a lot of lost time to make up for." She snuggled into his embrace, her lips brushing his neck. She inhaled his warm, clean scent, wanting to touch as much of him as she could.

Suddenly serious, he stroked her cheek with the back of his hand. "I don't think I can ever really make it up to you, but I'm willing to try. I meant everything I said. I want you back, and I'm ready to prove it to you."

"How would you do that?" Her tone was lighthearted, but her heart raced at the possibilities.

"I'll do whatever it takes to show you that I'm serious about this, about us." His voice never wavered, and he tilted her face so that their eyes met.

"Whatever it takes?" she squeezed the words out, wanting so badly to believe him.

But she'd been promised a future before, only to have him end things when she didn't follow him to Los Angeles.

When someone broke your heart after that, was it ever safe to let them back in? Was it fair to any relationship they might build to know that she would always remember the past? She had grown in the last decade, and much of that had been shaped by the people who had let her down. She had become a woman who owned her choices and made her own way in the world. There wasn't a doubt in her mind he was sincere this time around. The problem was that he was equally sincere the first time he promised her his heart.

"We could start with dinner. Let's order in," she suggested. She had huge decisions to make when it came to her future with Adam, but it wouldn't hurt to enjoy the evening.

• • •

Soft sunlight filtered through the blinds and curtains in Zoe's bedroom, waking him though he squeezed his eye closed against the light. Adam stretched, tangling the sheets around his waist, and smiled with satisfaction as the night before danced across his memory. He turned to face the bedside clock and sat straight up, his eyes scanning the room for his discarded clothes. Zoe was nowhere to be seen; she'd likely gone downstairs to open the bakery hours ago. He swung his legs over the side of the bed and raked his fingers through his disheveled hair. Last night couldn't have gone better if he had scripted it. She was amazing, everything he remembered and more than he dared hope for. Surely she would come around and see that he could be trusted this time. He found his clothes and dressed quickly, though he'd never make it on time to meet his father at the office.

Making his way through her apartment, he stepped into the bathroom and regarded himself in the mirror. He looked like a man who had been well and truly satisfied. She had kept him awake for hours after dinner last night, talking and making love, and he should be exhausted. Instead, he couldn't wipe the wide smile off of his face, and he couldn't remember the last time he'd felt like this, if he'd ever felt like this. It was as though he'd finally found the peace he didn't realize was missing in his life. Everything was falling into place, with Zoe at least. He knew he had to make major decisions when it came to his job, his home, and the farm, but it wouldn't hurt to enjoy the moment. He couldn't find a spare toothbrush, so he twisted the lid off of the bottle of blue mouthwash he found on her counter and swished a swig around his mouth.

Her bathroom was like the rest of her apartment—tidy and spare but essentially Zoe. Her methodical, purposeful life was reflected in the items she chose to surround herself with. Nothing was extraneous and everything was beautiful, as though chosen with care. Even her towels and soaps were a soft shade of blush pink that matched the rugs and curtains. Her appreciation of small details was evident in her home and work. It was such a stark contrast to her upbringing when her parents' alcohol use and general laziness meant that, more often than not, her clothes were shabby and mismatched and she may not always have dinner prepared for her at home. He wondered if her new life was a conscious departure from her youth.

Despite the allure of grown-up Zoe's apartment and all it represented, he had a meeting with his father and couldn't dawdle. He made his way to her living room, pausing outside her bedroom door one last time to spare a glance at the bed. Her soft sheets were twisted, and her comforter had been kicked to the floor. His heart squeezed and his body stirred, warmed at the memory of the night before. He found his shoes and pushed his feet inside, wanting to linger but needing to leave. He took the stairs down to the street and went into the bakery from the front entrance.

Courtney was behind the counter, ringing up a customer's purchase. She flashed him a knowing smile. "Good morning." She handed the customer's change over and cocked her thumb toward the back door. "Zoe's baking, so you can just go on back."

He thanked her and ducked past the curious stares of the few customers who likely either knew who he was or were still trying to place him. He pushed the door open and a wall of warm, fragrant air met him. Zoe was sliding a silver baking tray of pastries into the oven; she gave him a welcoming grin as he entered.

"Good morning, sleepyhead." Her dark hair was pulled up into a neat bun, and her pink apron was already dusted with flour. Her cheeks flushed prettily from the oven's temperature, reminding him of the way her cheeks flushed the night before.

"Good morning, beautiful." He crossed the room to join her and softly kissed her forehead. "I thought I would find you down here. Can I help you with anything, bring you something?"

"I'm fine." She fished a key ring out of her pocket and pressed it into his palm. "You could lock up the apartment if you don't mind."

"Sure thing." He leaned down and kissed her cheek. "I'll leave the keys up front with Courtney; I've got to get back to the office. My dad's probably wondering where I am."

She stood on her toes and wrapped her arms around his shoulders, drawing him closer for a real kiss. Her lips were sweet, and he didn't hesitate when they opened beneath his to deepen the kiss. He could taste something like cinnamon, maybe apple, as their tongues found each other. Feeling his body respond to her closeness and that ubiquitous vanilla scent that surrounded her, he broke off the kiss and held her close for a moment before things could get out of hand. "If I don't go right now, I'm going to throw you over my shoulder and drag you back to your apartment," he teased, but it was halfway true.

"All right then, Romeo. Go see your dad and we'll catch up later." She gave him a playful slap on the backside and pushed him toward the side door. "Hey," she said, and he paused with his hand on the doorknob.

"Yes?"

"Thank you for last night. It was really something special." Her voice was soft, shy, but her eyes twinkled with affection.

He shook his head and blew out a breath. "Last night was incredible. I hope it was just the first of many to come."

He left before he got pulled back into her orbit.

• • •

Zoe pushed through the kitchen door carrying a tray of freshly baked pear pastries and opened the back of the display case. Her night with Adam and his visit this morning pleasantly distracted her from the mundane tasks of work, and she knew the dreamy smile on her face would give her away, but couldn't help herself. She placed each pastry on a crisp individual paper doily and lined them up neatly in the case. Courtney had kept the bakery clean during the first morning rush, so Zoe had plenty of time to wander around the shop, straightening inventory or adding special touches to her displays. The shelves holding Emerald Tea had never looked better; she found herself straightening the packets for sale, and refreshing the sample bar more often since Adam was back in her life. It was silly, but having the tea in her shop was a tangible reminder of their new alliance.

The lone customer still lingering over tea and a cherry pastry finally finished her morning meal and left the shop. At the sound of the door's bell, Courtney made a beeline to Zoe, eyes sparkling with amusement.

"Oh my gosh, you have to tell me what's going on with you and Adam Whitman. He looked positively edible this morning. You can't tell me it's nothing." Courtney put her hands on her hips and waited. "Spill it, sister."

She laughed then sent a quick glance toward the door. Nobody was coming in, and Adam had been more than clear about his intentions. Courtney didn't need to know the specifics, not that she had any, but it couldn't hurt anything to share a little information. "All right, fine," she said as she led Courtney to a table and took a seat across from her. "I guess you could say we're getting back together."

"I kind of assumed that, from the looks of him when he came down from your apartment this morning." Courtney gave her a meaningful look. "So how is this going to work? He doesn't live here, does he?"

"We haven't really talked about the specifics too much." She chewed on her lip. "Richard wants him to take over the farm so he can retire, so I hope that Adam is planning on doing that. He'd have to quit his job in L.A., sell his condo, and move here, but I don't see how else it could work."

"That would be a really big change."

Zoe's optimism faded a bit as Courtney's statement echoed her own misgivings. He had never outlined his specific plans, and she feared he hadn't thought it through as much as he wanted to believe. Was he really interested in taking over the family farm? Was he ready to commit to her this time? It was one thing to enjoy their rekindled affection for one another, and she had no doubt that he was sincere—he had his faults but he wasn't one to lead a girl on. He likely believed every word he said, even if he hadn't thought things out. She couldn't ignore the nagging fear that once he really started making plans for the future, something would happen to derail them. "It would be a big change. I guess we'll just have to take things as they come." She traced the scratches on the table with a fingertip.

"He seems to be really into you. Every time he steps foot through that door, whatever girls are here practically give themselves whiplash, and he doesn't notice anybody but you."

She smiled at that. "Oh, yeah?"

"Yeah. Plus, he's the reason the case was practically empty. He bought half the pastries before he left this morning."

"So that's what happened. I wondered if we were running a sale I didn't know about," she joked. "We'd better get a move on if we're going to have enough for the next rush." The ladies rose and propped the kitchen door open so they could bake and listen for customers. Everything Nice always enjoyed a second wave of customers they lovingly dubbed the mommy crowd: young mothers who enjoyed pastries and tea while they chatted. Courtney created fruity iced tea blends without caffeine for the kids, and they could expect both moms and toddlers to be content to linger throughout the morning. It was great for business, and Zoe looked forward to seeing the children every morning. She tried not to think about whether adorable children of her own were in her future.

The kneading, mixing, and assembling as she worked side by side with Courtney took her mind off of her misgivings and allowed her to simply bask in her reconnection with Adam. Surely it was better to enjoy what they had rather than to spend so much time worrying about what was to come, but there was too much history between them to pretend she was confident when she wasn't.

Ashley poked her head around the doorframe and Zoe looked up from their work, surprised neither of them had heard the door. "Good morning, ladies."

She wiped her hands off on her apron and crossed the kitchen to meet Ashley, while Courtney finished sliding the pastries into the oven and worked on cleaning up the kitchen. "Good morning."

Ashley had come at the same time every morning for months to pick up the food for the Senior Day Center. Zoe stacked the pink bakery boxes on the counter as Ashley poured herself a cup of tea. "So, I saw Adam this morning before I left the office. He brought breakfast for everyone."

"Ah, that makes sense. I wondered why he would buy out most of my inventory, and there's no way one man can eat as much as he took. We're scrambling to get ready for the mommy crowd." She poured her own tea and sat with Ashley.

"I wonder how he got over here early enough to buy pastries before hitting the office." Ashley blew on her tea and gave her a mischievous look.

"Who knows?" she said with a laugh. She sipped her tea and hoped Ashley wouldn't ask her anything too personal. They had been friends for a long time, and through their work they had become closer than ever. Still, she wasn't sure if she was ready to spill the intimate details of their night together yet.

"So what's the deal with you two? I've never seen Adam like this before." Ashley tapped the contents of a sugar packet into her cup and stirred.

She straightened her back and leaned forward on her elbows. "Like what?"

"You know," Ashley said with a wave of her hand. "So interested in everything. He usually comes home for holidays, sticks around long enough to visit with everybody, and then he's off again. He's been out on the farm, all over the offices, and of course, over here with you this time and it's different. That's all."

"I know. I mean, I guess I don't really know, since in the past he's done a great job of avoiding me every time he comes to town." Unable to keep it a secret, she looked down into her cup and said, "He wants to get back together."

Ashley's forehead furrowed. "It's kind of sudden, don't you think?"

Her heart fell. Hearing her fears echoed back to her chilled her. "That's what I've been afraid of."

"It might be just fine, nothing to be afraid of. Has he made any plans?"

"I guess, sort of. He hasn't told Richard he'll take over the farm, but I know he has spent hours with him getting familiar with the business."

"But what about quitting his job, moving here? He can always stay in the old house while he looks for a place here, but that's not a permanent solution."

She buried her face in her hands. "It's like you're reading my mind. I've thought the same things. I just didn't want to acknowledge it."

Ashley reached across the table and touched her arm, a sympathetic look on her face. "I don't want to discourage you if you're happy. Maybe I shouldn't have brought it up."

"It's fine, really. I wouldn't be so upset if I hadn't thought the same things myself. Why am I so willing to just fall back into a relationship with him? He still has a home and a job in California! He doesn't even live here."

"If he says he wants to get back together, I'm sure he means it. Maybe you could give him a chance to prove he's sincere. I mean, you've been apart for years, so what's a little more time to let him show you he means what he says?"

"At my age, if things don't move along quickly, I'll miss out on a lot. I don't know if he wants to have kids, or even if he wants to get married, now that I think about it. I'm starting to wonder if this is a bad idea, if maybe I shouldn't start over with someone new. Someone who hasn't broken my heart already."

"You know, I see where you're coming from, and I totally understand, but it might be a little hasty to dismiss the whole thing with Adam. Why don't you wait and see what he does? If he's as serious as he thinks he is, he'll quit his job in L.A. and find a place here. I really think that he is sincere, but meaning something and following through are two different things."

"That's true. He can't have that much more time off from work. Surely he's got to do something soon, whether it's go back or quit. I guess I'll know what he's going to do soon enough."

Ashley sat up and finished her tea. "Absolutely. I don't think he's lying when he says he wants to get back together, but he might not have really thought things through. Give him a chance to show you one way or the other before you throw the whole thing out."

"You're absolutely right. I can't sit around wringing my hands and worrying that he's not coming back. I'll just wait and see."

"Sounds like a plan." Ashley patted her hand and stood up. "I've got to get over to the Senior Day Center and then back to the office. Call me if you need me."

Ashley threw her empty cup into the garbage can and balanced the bakery boxes in her arms. Zoe opened the door for her friend and said goodbye. However, Ashley's words hung in the air, thick and ugly. Adam might not have a reason to lie, but this wasn't the first time they'd been in this situation. If she were smart, she'd get out while her heart was still intact.

Chapter Ten

Zoe strode into the farm's stock building, humming to herself. After a good night's sleep, she'd decided to take Adam at his word until he gave her reason not to. Sitting around, fretting, waiting for him to disappoint her did nothing but waste time, and she had work to do. Ashley was chewing on her lip and staring at the clipboard in her hands when Zoe walked in. The serene music and heavenly aroma of the teas on the shelves seemed at odds with the nervous energy buzzing around the room. She cleared her throat and Ashley finally looked up.

"Hey," Ashley said with a breathless voice. "I didn't hear you come in. My mind is everywhere this morning."

Zoe set her bag down on the counter and approached her friend. "What's going on?"

"Things are going crazy around here. Somebody ran a truck or something over the fencing that separates Emerald Tea from Split Acres, and the whole thing's just ruined."

"Wow, any idea how it happened?"

Ashley shook her head. "Nope, and nobody's talking. Uncle Richard said he and Adam went by Split Acres last week and Colleen couldn't get them out of there fast enough, so he thinks that Joe Sanders might have a problem with him. I would be surprised if Joe actually did it, but there's nothing to say that someone from Split Acres isn't responsible. Uncle Richard is out there now assessing the damage, and until everything gets cleared up, we won't know what's going on. This could be a matter of simply rebuilding the fence or it could be worse."

"How could it be worse?" A wrecked fence and decimated grass seemed serious enough to her.

"Nobody checks the perimeter every day or anything. Uncle Richard is pretty sure it happened yesterday, but it could have been as many as three days ago. Without barriers, we don't know what has passed over the boundaries. They'll have to do a lot of testing to be sure the soil hasn't been contaminated, and even if everything else looks okay, the rest of the crops will need to be checked. Fortunately, they leave an acre between the farms to act as a buffer from the pesticides and chemicals on the Sanders farm, but you can't be too careful."

She cringed. "I didn't think of all that. What a mess."

"Yeah. It could mean a whole lot of trouble. Either way, there's a lot of work to be done to fix it."

"Do you know if Adam is out there now?"

"Probably. He and Uncle Richard left straight from the house to meet Jacob." Ashley wrinkled her nose in distaste. Jacob Sanders was a couple of years behind Zoe in school, but he'd grown up with Ashley. "I had to come in a little early to open the offices and fill everyone in."

"I'm going to go see if I can help with anything." Zoe picked her bag up from the counter.

"All right, just call me if they need something from here."

"Sure. I'll swing back by later to pick up my order."

• • •

A few minutes later, Zoe pulled up to the border fence between the Whitman farm and Split Acres and parked next to Richard's truck and a car from the sheriff's department. The fence began at the acre-wide buffer zone between the two farms, where the Whitmans had a wide swath of nothing but grass, which she now knew was to ensure that chemicals from the neighboring farm didn't seep into the soil and affect the organic crops. Muddy tire tracks snaked through the grass, crisscrossing as if the driver went through the grass, backed up, went around, and had another go.

What a mess. She made her way to the men, watching her step to stay out of the mud and avoid tripping over the deep ruts.

Jacob Sanders, the local sheriff's deputy and son of Richard's former partner, stood with Adam and Richard. The three men held identical stances: hands on hips, eyes squinted as they surveyed the damage. Zoe couldn't hear what they were saying, but she guessed it was bad, as Richard gestured out into the distance then wiped his brow. Adam looked up and noticed her approach, and the other men's heads swiveled in her direction. She raised her hand in a tentative wave, and Adam left the trio to meet her. He softly kissed her forehead and pressed his face to the top of her head, breathing her in.

With his arms wrapped around her, his voice rumbled in his chest against her cheek as he spoke. "Hey, what are you doing out here?"

She pulled back and looked up. "Ashley told me what happened, so I drove out to see if either of you needed anything."

He released her from the embrace and took her hand, walking with her to join Jacob and Richard. "I can't think of anything."

She exchanged greetings with the other men. The tension in the air was thick, almost palpable. With the Whitmans' suspicions of Joe, having his son working the scene was awkward. Had he made any progress on finding the identity of the Immigration imposters? How much of their run-in with Colleen the other day did Jacob know about? A nagging thought tugged at her, one she didn't voice. Her father worked at Split Acres and didn't exactly have a pristine driving record. If Marlon was the culprit, it was likely an accident, but with his misguided sense of entitlement, she could never know for sure.

"Zoe just stopped by to see if she could help out somehow, but I can't think of anything. Dad?"

Richard looked like he was going to say no, but then snapped his finger and nodded. "We left the house so fast this morning when we got the call that I left something behind. I need to get a package in the mail to the IRS today, and I don't know when I'll get back to the house. Would you mind picking it up and dropping it off at the post office? I wouldn't ask, but it's really important."

"Sure, absolutely, no problem."

He checked his watch. "Patty should still be there for a couple of hours at least, so you can get in. I'll call her so she can have it ready for you when you get there. It's a bright green envelope, already addressed and stamped. You can't miss it."

"No problem. I'm going to work after I leave the post office, so just call me if you need anything else. Courtney's working all day so I can come back if you need me." Zoe jangled her car keys and gave Adam a quick kiss before leaving the men and driving across town to Richard's house.

• • •

Patty opened the door for Zoe and ushered her inside, talking as she walked. "How were they? Richard was so worried when they left this morning."

"Jacob Sanders was with them, and they all seemed pretty calm. They didn't give me any details, but it seemed like they were okay." Zoe wandered into the kitchen's cozy breakfast nook, her eyes passing over papers with the Eco Initiatives letterhead scattered as though Adam had been reading when they got the phone call. His laptop sat open in front of a kitchen chair, and before she could stop herself, Zoe moved the mouse until the monitor lit up.

Patty bustled in and examined the table, her brows knitted. "Richard said the package would be here, but I don't see a green envelope anywhere, do you?" When Zoe shook her head, she continued. "Let me check around a bit before we bother him. Make yourself at home."

Left alone, Zoe indulged her curiosity, though her intuition told her she'd be better off respecting Adam's privacy. His email was open to the message he'd been reading when they left, and the air left her lungs as she scanned the text. He had been exchanging emails about a promotion, when he expected to be back in the office, whether he'd had time to consider an offer. The papers scattered on the table held information about compensation, benefits, new job responsibilities, a new title. She picked one up that looked like an official job offer. Not only was he not closer to quitting his job and taking over the farm, he was heading in the opposite direction. Her heart sank, and her throat tightened as tears threatened to spill over her lashes. The hand holding the paper shook violently as Zoe wrestled with her anger, disappointment, and sadness. If she could hold it together long enough to get the package and leave, she'd allow the tears to flow in the car. If Patty came in and saw her upset, there would be no way around a long heart-to-heart talk, and Zoe simply wasn't ready to share her feelings yet. Where was Patty with that package?

"Here you go." Patty bustled in, carrying a bright green envelope.

"Thanks. I'll get it to the post office right away."

"Thank you. I'm sure Richard appreciates you doing this for him. He rushed out of here so quickly this morning that he just left it behind. It's already late, you know."

Sure that Patty would notice her trembling, she tucked the envelope under her arm and pasted a pleasant smile on her face. "I'll go right now."

Before the housekeeper could engage her any further, Zoe hurried out to her car and enclosed herself in the blessed silence. After a few deep, calming breaths, she pulled out of the driveway, determined not to break down where Patty could look out the window and see her. She drove through Richard's neighborhood, choking back the tears until they overtook her and she was forced to pull over by a neighborhood park. With a shuddering breath, she finally allowed herself to feel the emotion she'd been holding back. Without an audience, her tears became sobs—ugly, loud sobs that wracked her body. How had she let herself fall for Adam again so quickly, and what made her think he had changed? He was just as focused on his career as ever, probably more so now that he'd be taking on more responsibility. What had the papers said? That he'd be responsible for accounts in the entire state. How long had he known about the promotion?

His sweet words, the ease with which she slipped back into a relationship with him, how close she'd come to admitting that she loved him. Zoe clutched her stomach. Hunched over, she wailed in the closed car, giving voice to her pain. It was time she severed the ties that held her so close to Adam. He'd run roughshod over her feelings one too many times, and she wouldn't be the naïve girl waiting for him to come around this time.

• • •

"So, you'll keep us updated with any leads?" Adam asked Jacob Sanders after he'd finished taking notes. "We'll want to get the repairs underway immediately so we don't lose too much production time on our side of the fence."

"Uh, yeah, Adam, I'll contact the office when I've filed the report. We'll keep in contact." Jacob looked confused, and Adam knew that he was probably wondering why it was he and not his father taking charge of the discussion.

When they'd received the call about the damaged fence, Adam's thoughts immediately went to the problems it could cause, from the testing that would be required, to the potential loss of production due to cross-contamination. It was then that he'd decided to turn down the promotion at Eco Initiatives and commit to Emerald Tea Farm. He knew more about farming than he'd previously thought, and now he could finally admit to himself that he wanted to learn more. He wanted to take the business to the next level of environmental responsibility, he wanted to expand their operations, and he wanted to build the family legacy. He wanted to be in Emerald Springs to protect the businesses that couldn't afford to protect themselves against con artists like the Immigration agent imposters. And more than anything, he wanted to marry Zoe Miller.

His phone buzzed, and he recognized the Eco Initiatives number. "Adam Whitman."

"Adam, hi, it's Mark Campbell. I know you're on vacation, so I hope this isn't a bad time." The Eco Initiatives senior partner's tone told him that it didn't matter if it was a bad time or not.

"No, of course not, Mr. Campbell. What can I do for you?"

"I just got off the phone with Christine Grazioli, and I'm concerned about our agreement with Everlight Optics."

"I met with her personally before I left town, and she was all set to sign and get started."

"Well, she hasn't signed yet. I'm worried that if you don't work some of your Adam Whitman magic on her, she's not going to."

Crap. Even though his heart was already in Emerald Springs, Adam didn't want to leave his old job in disarray. The Everlight deal was huge for Eco Initiatives, and he would see it through. "All right, I'll come back early. Give me a little time to change my flight, and I'll be on my way."

Chapter Eleven

The afternoon crowd had thinned out, and Courtney had the front covered, so Zoe was free to hole up in her office and finish paperwork. With Adam back in her life, she had let the busy work of her business slide lately. With the pain of her discovery still fresh, she was more determined than ever to take control. Nobody else had ever taken care of her, and nobody was going to start now. She was responsible for her life and her business, and she wouldn't be distracted by the heartache Adam couldn't help but cause. Her office phone rang, snapping her to attention.

"Everything Nice." She hoped her voice was sunnier than her outlook.

"Zoe." Adam's rich baritone still stirred her, and she hated herself for it.

"Hey," she said, careful to reveal nothing. As far as he knew, everything was still wonderful between them.

"Can I pick you up? I need to see you."

"Sure. Courtney can close the shop, and we are pretty much empty here." She sat up straight and ran her fingers through her hair. Her body strummed with tension at the thought of seeing him again, but the sooner he revealed his intentions the better.

"All right, I'll come right over. See you in a few." For a fleeting moment, she thought she heard seriousness in his tone that matched her own black mood but dismissed it.

Attempting to distract herself, she tidied up her desk and freshened up her makeup. Her shirt was smudged with icing, so she pulled a clean t-shirt out of a stack she kept in her office and changed, satisfied that her casual dress would be fine for a last-minute outing. Her hair was full and wavy after being curled into her customary tight bun all day, and he loved running his fingers through her hair when it was down. It was time she stopped thinking of him and the things he loved to do to her. She headed for the front to wait for Adam and help Courtney until she left, ready to face him with aplomb.

As she was scribbling the last item on a list of things to do the next morning, Adam came into view through the shop's window. Her breath caught in her throat at the sight of him—how long would it take to get over him this time? Their eyes met, and she made her way around the counter to meet him. His expression was serious, sending tension racing through her. Zoe stepped out onto the sidewalk, into the humid summer air, and turned her face so that his kiss landed on her cheek.

"Can I buy you a drink, or is it too early?" If he noticed her acting strangely, he didn't let on.

She checked her watch and shrugged, thinking a cold beer would make the bad news go down easier anyway. "Sure, why not?"

He placed a gentle hand at the small of her back, and they walked down Spruce Street toward The Rusty Tap. The soft sunshine and bustling activity downtown mocked Zoe with their happiness. He didn't have to say anything to make her feel like she was walking to the gallows. After reading the papers and his email, she figured this last-minute outing was surely where he would drop the bomb on her that he was leaving again. As much as she wanted to pull away and run back home, it was best to get it over with.

He pulled the door to the bar open for her and they stepped inside, instantly enveloped in the bar's dim light and stagnant air. Her eyes adjusted, and she blinked as she looked around the old, rundown interior. She rarely drank alcohol, but she'd made the occasional exception, going for drinks with friends or gathering for celebrations, and more recently her dates with Adam. Today her mood was just as dreary as place itself. He led her through the bar, their feet sticking a little on the threadbare carpet, past the tables scattered around the middle of the room, to a booth in a dark corner. A single pendant lamp illuminated the scarred, greasy table that sat between two red vinyl-covered booth seats. They slid into their seats and Zoe craned her neck to see if a waitress was serving patrons or if they were on their own.

He scooted across the booth and touched her hand lightly. "Is beer okay? I can grab a pitcher."

"Sure, that sounds great." She doubted the bar stocked wine, and if they did it probably came in a box. A sudsy, cheap beer would go perfectly with the angst-ridden nineties alternative rock song drifting out of the jukebox. She offered him a weak smile and watched him walk to the bar, noting the curious looks from the few other women. He never looked at another girl when they were together, not even when he was across the room from her. His jeans hugged his muscles as he leaned against the bar and talked with the bartender, and she gave herself a mental slap for even noticing. Chances were good that things with Adam would end today. With a pitcher of beer in one hand and a couple of glasses in the other, he made his way back to their table.

"You know that guy? I think we went to high school with him." He jerked his head toward the bartender as he slid into the booth. "He seemed to know me, so I just went with it." He poured beer for both of them and slid a glass over to her.

She sipped the cold brew and relaxed into her seat, deciding then that one beer would be her limit. Pairing alcohol with tough conversations was asking for trouble. "Everybody knows you. Face it, you can't go anywhere in this town without getting recognized, and when you take charge of the farm, it'll get worse."

A looked passed across his face so quickly Zoe wasn't sure what she'd seen, but her heart sank. He shifted uncomfortably in his seat and trained his eyes on the table as he took a sip of his beer. His gaze drifted out around the bar, anywhere but across the table at her. "I might as well just come out with it. No use dragging things out too much."

"What is it?" She was ready for this, but her heart raced and she steeled herself for what was coming next.

"I need to head back to L.A. for a while. I've got a work thing to sort out, and then I can come back."

Her body trembled; anger stuck in her throat. Was this it? Was he really going to dismiss her without even mentioning the huge promotion? How dare he? Mentally calming herself, deciding to rein in her fury and give him a chance to explain, she took a long pull from her glass. Centered again and determined to handle the situation with grace, she forced a smile and injected as much light into her voice as she could. "Okay, so what's the plan?"

"I don't really have a specific plan yet. Something big has come up at one of my major accounts and I need to go sort it out. I should only be a little while."

"How will this work out if you want us to get back together?" Her anger was rising again, and she mentally tamped it down. No need to freak out just yet—there was still time for him to come clean.

He exhaled audibly, looking as though his thoughts were anywhere but with her. "I'm going to quit, and then I can firm up the timeline with my dad for taking over the farm. I know it's bad timing for us, but we have the rest of our lives to sort things out. The sooner I get back to L.A., the sooner I can come back home to you."

"I guess I don't understand. You say you're going to quit your job, but you don't have any sort of plan. Going home to work on some project doesn't make a lot of sense if you're leaving." Tears brimmed in her eyes, and her heart sank. If he went to Los Angeles, she didn't trust him to come back. It was too soon to test their new relationship, and her doubts about him grew with every moment he failed to disclose the promotion.

"I don't want to leave Eco Initiatives on bad terms, and trust me, if I leave them hanging, I'll be leaving on bad terms." He sounded almost glib, with a light laugh in his voice, an affectation that hadn't been there before. Was he reverting to his old self before he had even left Washington? Was this his L.A. persona? She didn't know what he was doing, but she didn't like it.

"Adam, I still haven't been able to decide if you're serious about us or not, whether I should trust you or cut my losses and move on. If you leave now, when things are so tenuous between us, it could be a disaster." It hurt to admit her fears and insecurities, to chance losing everything, but she couldn't take another heartbreak.

"It won't be a disaster. Things are going great, and when I get back it'll be like nothing happened." His voice was soft, gentle, but she didn't feel the confidence he tried to project.

"Maybe, maybe not. At this point, I don't even believe you will come back. I don't understand why you are so willing to leave town when everything is so new with us, when I am right here in front of you telling you how scared it makes me."

"I'm sitting here telling you I'll come back."

"Don't sound so surprised. The last time you left, you promised me you'd be back to start our life together. You'll remember how that turned out." Knowing he had a huge secret, one he hadn't so much as mentioned to her, told her everything she needed to know.

"I do remember how that turned out. I also remember how you were ready to join me in L.A., so you could support me and we could be together. You'll remember how that turned out." His voice was low, almost cold.

"How dare you? My dad needed me!"

He slapped his palm to the table. "I needed you, Zoe! That was your choice, not mine. You could have come to L.A., found a great job, and we could have been married. Letting go was your choice."

She shredded a bar napkin, keeping her eyes trained on her hands. True, it had been her decision, but her father's depression terrified her at the time. She wouldn't have been able to live with herself if something had happened to him after she left Emerald Springs. Adam had shown so little interest in her work and dreams, she'd been afraid to take the chance, to give up the security of her community and family only to risk having him lose interest in her.

"I need you to believe in me." He kept his eyes wide, refusing to look away.

"If you are really sincere, then just quit your job in L.A. and take over Emerald Tea Farm. People quit jobs all the time; this isn't exactly a moral issue or anything. It's not like there won't be someone else there to take over for you."

He sputtered, obviously not sure what to say to that. "Zoe, I ... listen, if I can't go back to tie up some loose ends without you thinking I might not come back, then we have big problems."

"Can you blame me? This is the same situation we were in fifteen years ago, only this time I know better than to just take you at your word. I know you've been spending a lot of time with your dad, but have you thought about selling your condo, have you quit your job, have you given any thought to where you'll live when you come back here?"

"Zoe, please." His voice was low, rough.

"Have you?" Her voice cracked as the tears finally spilled over her lashes and landed in fat puddles on the table, mixing with the condensation ring from her drink.

"No." The word was almost a whisper.

"Then I can't believe you're serious about us, and we're through until you make some solid plans. If you leave without knowing what's coming next, I'll drive myself crazy thinking it's going to be just like it was before. I'm sorry, so sorry, but I can't risk my heart again." Her chest constricted, and for a moment, no air could squeeze into her lungs.

"Zoe, please. Wait." He reached across the table and grasped her hands in his.

"I need you to stay, or at least resign and only go back so you can move."

"You know, you're not the only one in this relationship. You're asking me to give up everything—my home, the job I've worked for, the progress I've made. Maybe I should ask you to sell your bakery and move to L.A. with me. You could just as easily open your own business there."

"What?"

"Sounds crazy, right? Well, think about it. You're asking me to blow off everything I've worked for with a phone call." He paused, his eyes flashing with anger. "And we both know how much you hate ending things with phone calls."

"I know about the promotion."

"What?"

"When I went to your dad's house, I saw your papers and your emails about it. I didn't mean to snoop. I just saw it. Were you going to tell me?"

He raked a hand through his hair and blew out a long, slow breath as his eyes scanned the room. "I don't know. I guess I was thinking I'd figure out everything on my own and you wouldn't need to know about it."

"Are you still considering it?" Her voice was little more than a whisper, and she couldn't meet his eyes.

"No. Everything I want is here."

"Then why can't you make a plan? This feels worse than the last time because now I know what it's like to lose you. I need more than words, I need a plan. I'm sorry, but that's the only way I'll know you're serious. Can you do that?" Pleased to have taken control of her own life, Zoe sat up straight and waited for his answer.

"Come on." His eyes pleaded with her, but his answer was not yes.

"I can't do this. Last time, I gave you the power to hold my heart in your hands and you crushed it."

"You think you're the only one who was hurt? Come on, Zoe. You went to culinary school; you could've worked anywhere in the world! You didn't have your own place, but somehow staying here was more important than our relationship."

"But, my dad—"

"Yeah, sure, your dad. After being here this week, I can understand why you didn't want to leave him, but you didn't even research your options. I think he was just your excuse to stay."

"Adam, come on."

"No, you come on. You cling to this idea that everything is my fault, but you've got to see that you could've made it work as well. You either didn't trust me and our relationship enough to take a chance and move, or you just didn't care enough. Either way, I'm not the only one at fault here."

"All I know is that I can't survive getting over you again. Goodbye, Adam." Her voice was stronger than she felt. Though she knew it was the right decision, her heart cracked open as she spoke. On wobbly legs, she stood and rushed out of the bar, her vision blurred with tears.

• • •

Adam sat at their table, sipping his beer and seething. Watching her walk away was like a punch in the gut, until he recovered from the shock and indignation which settled over him like a blanket wrapped around his shoulders. He was thirty-three years old and had a career, an important career, and he wasn't going to let anyone else dictate how he would handle ending it. He had lived and breathed Eco Initiatives for the last decade of his life, dedicating his entire professional focus to the company and its mission. Leaving it behind wasn't something that would be accomplished with a phone call. He owed it to himself, to his colleagues and clients, to tie up loose ends. He would leave his position better than he found it, his legacy intact. He tipped his glass and drained the last of his beer, enjoying the warmth that spread through his limbs.

• • •

A week later, Adam was back at his desk at Eco Initiatives, catching up on the backlog of work waiting for him. The office lights threatened to give him a migraine as he tried to focus on the papers stacked on his desk and the emails he'd yet to read. As annoying as it was, at least the unrelenting background noise helped drown out some of the heartache of his last conversation with Zoe.

When she said they were through, she clearly meant it. She'd steadfastly refused to take his calls or see him since their discussion. He hated leaving town with things between them so broken, but what else could he do if she wouldn't talk to him? He'd thought of little else since the night she left, but he couldn't let her insecurity determine his actions. His fingers danced over the packet containing his offer letter. All it needed was a signature and he would be head of operations for the entire state, a feat practically unheard of at his age. He was ready for it, though. He had the education, the experience, and the connections to almost guarantee success. So why hadn't he signed the paper and accepted the promotion? He already decided that he wouldn't live in Emerald Springs and run the farm without Zoe in his life, and she'd let him go at the first hint of uncertainty.

"Knock, knock," a female singsong voice came from his doorway. Christine from Everlight Optics poked her head around the door and caught his eye. "Hi, Adam."

"Good morning, Christine. Come on in." He rose as she walked in and he shook her hand, leaning across his desk. She seated herself in one of the chairs opposite his as he sat.

"I never heard back from you after our meeting, so I thought it was time for a visit."

"I was called out of town on family business, but came back as soon as I heard you needed to see me. I'm so sorry that you were waiting, but it wasn't necessary. Any of our associates can handle your paperwork." He had done the legwork to close the deal, but the account would belong to Eco Initiatives, not him alone.

"I got everything right after our last meeting, and I'm sure someone would've been happy to help me. But I don't want someone from the office to handle it. I want you … " she smiled knowingly and paused, "to handle it."

Without thinking, he mirrored her smile and leaned forward on his elbows. Realizing what he was doing, he cleared his throat, sat back in his chair, and stopped his automatic flirtation response. Had he been doing this for so long that it was second nature? He had always told himself he made deals because of his knowledge and experience, his innovative ideas, not his charisma. His relationships were professional, weren't they? "Let's see," he murmured as he tapped on his keyboard. "I can print out your agreement and we can get you started right away. Just as soon as you sign, I'll get your account set up for service and you will be on your way to putting our plans in motion." His tone was professional, offering no hint of flirtation.

"Why don't you just meet me for dinner tonight and bring it with you? I can sign it then." She was practically purring, and Adam felt bile rise in his throat. This was not the life he was supposed to be living.

"Ms. Grazioli, I apologize, but will you excuse me? I'm not feeling well." He stood and loosened his tie, the air in his office suddenly too warm and still for comfort. "I'll send an associate in to help you."

Without waiting for an answer, he rushed out of his office and down the hall to the men's room. After splashing cold water on his face, he braced himself on the cool porcelain sink and stared at his reflection in the mirror. He'd let ambition and pride rule his life for far too long. So what if Zoe demanded more from him? Didn't she have every reason and right? How had he let her walk away that night without more of a fight? It disgusted him to think he was so focused on himself and this job that he refused to listen. All he'd heard was an ultimatum when she was more likely begging him to put her first for once. To put his money where his mouth was so to speak. He didn't blame her one bit for not believing him. If he were brutally honest with himself, he hadn't yet given serious enough consideration to actually quitting his job, moving back, taking over the farm. The only thing he'd ever been sure about was Zoe, and he'd let her slip through his fingers … *again*.

It couldn't be too late. Hoping his office would be empty when he returned, he strode down the hallway, focused on tendering his resignation and putting the plans in motion to return to Emerald Springs and Zoe.

• • •

"Have you talked to Adam since he left?" Ashley wrapped her hands around a cup of hot tea and leaned forward on her elbows.

"No, I was waiting to see if he really follows through this time." Zoe busied herself with wiping down the already-clean beverage station. "I'm starting to wonder if that's a good idea."

"Oh?" Ashley raised her eyebrows, but there was no judgment in her tone.

Zoe bit her lip, concentrating even more closely on her cleaning. She'd been full of righteous indignation at the discovery of Adam's potential promotion and his refusal to make satisfactory plans. She hadn't expected his angry reaction, though, and his refusal to shoulder all the blame for their troubles had thrown her for a loop. For years, she'd held tightly to the certainty that she was left by Adam Whitman, that he'd been the one who ended their relationship.

"He was pretty angry when he left, and it got me to thinking." Zoe put her cleaning supplies under the cabinet and sat across from Ashley. "For as long as I can remember, I've told myself that our relationship ended because of Adam, and I never considered that it could've been my fault, too."

"Yeah, I've always wondered why you didn't move to L.A. with him." Ashley took a sip of her tea, looking like she worried how Zoe would react to that.

She sighed and traced her fingers along the scratches in the tabletop. "A lot of reasons, really, but when it comes down to it, I didn't trust the relationship enough and I was afraid to let go of what I knew. I've been so stupid."

Ashley reached across the table and laid her hand on Zoe's arm. "I'm sure you still have a chance to fix this."

"You think?"

"Absolutely. I see how Adam looks at you, and he is clearly a man in love. Plus, I've never seen him so involved with the business. He's been with Uncle Richard nonstop, and I know they've been working closely together. If you let him slip through your fingers this time, it really will be your fault."

Ashley's tone was light, but her meaning was clear. Zoe had taken the Whitman's support for granted for so long she'd allowed herself to feel infallible when it came to Adam. He was right, she could've worked anywhere, and the only things keeping her in Emerald Springs were her excuses. She wouldn't make the same mistake this time.

Chapter Twelve

Adam pulled into the farm's parking lot, barely taking the time to slam the car into park before throwing the door open. He switched off the engine, yanked the keys from the ignition, and hopped out, catching his arm on the seatbelt as he twisted out of the car. The two weeks that had passed between the moment he realized he would return home and take over his dad's position and when he actually set foot back in Emerald Springs had stretched out interminably. He couldn't get his plans in motion fast enough, since he couldn't share any of it with Zoe, and the wait to see how she'd react was agonizing. He'd called her, shaking with excitement over sharing his plans, but she didn't return that voice mail either. He'd recruited his family to expedite his return so he could leave as soon as his two weeks at work were up. He only had to ask, and his brothers flew to Los Angeles to help him pack his things and get his condo ready to put on the market. Without Daniel, it would have taken him twice as long to get everything in order. His brother had a gift for organization and efficiency. Chad was tireless, offering his muscle and stamina to pack and load endless boxes of Adam's belongings and move them into storage. Having his brothers come together so willingly to help him return home made it clear that he was making the right decision. He belonged in Emerald Springs as CEO of Emerald Tea Farm, and with any luck, married to Zoe Miller.

If he could actually find her, everything would be perfect; surely it would fall in place when she saw that he'd returned. She wasn't at her apartment or her shop, and of course, Courtney was close-lipped. He shook his head and smiled to himself. Women. Didn't she know he was back to make things right? He walked across the lot to the supply building and stepped into the tea-scented room.

Ashley and Zoe turned in unison from stocking the shelves, their eyes flying open in surprise. Ashley whipped her head around to see Zoe's reaction, and Zoe stood rooted in place, her face frozen in shock. He closed the distance between them, and she'd recovered enough to rearrange her features into a neutral expression. He was inches away from her, so close he could smell her familiar vanilla and sugar scent and feel the faint warmth from her skin. Goose bumps erupted on her arms left bare in a sleeveless red dress, her tiny waist cinched by a black patent leather belt. She raised her face to his but gave nothing away with her expression; her eyes remained passive, her lips closed. She didn't step back or move away from him, so he forged ahead.

He could handle anything she threw at him. She might want to push him away; she might even want to slap him. There was nothing left but to take the chance. "You said the only way you'd take me seriously was if I quit my job."

"Yes, but you don't have to do that. I was selfish, and it was wrong. I want to be with you, and it doesn't matter where we are as long as we're together."

"You said you wouldn't wait around for me to decide."

"That's true, but I will."

"I quit my job, and I'm moving back to Emerald Springs. I'm back for good. So much happened after I got back to L.A., but none of it meant anything to me when I couldn't share it with you."

"What do you mean?"

"My first day back in the office, I was practically buried under this pile of work that backed up while I was here, and I hated it. In the past, I would have relished getting back into the thick of it. You know, I loved working there. It was never just a job for me. That huge promotion? I would've given anything for it a month ago, but I couldn't bring myself to accept it."

"So what happened?"

"Once the initial excitement of the offer wore off, I realized I didn't care. I didn't want it because everything I care about is here. The only people and work that mean anything to me are here. I resigned right then and started getting ready to move back here."

Something like hope shined in her eyes. When she said she'd accept nothing less than total commitment, she was obviously prepared to follow through, and had. "You really resigned?"

"Yep. I am officially unemployed." He laughed and took her hand in his. "I couldn't wait to get back here to you, and you wouldn't even take my calls. I wanted so badly to tell you, to find out if there could still be a chance for us. It was an agonizing two weeks."

"I'm sorry," she whispered, sounding choked. "I had no right to demand you give up everything. Whatever we need to do to be together, we'll do. It's not all up to me. I didn't understand how much your job meant to you until I thought about what it would feel like to give up mine. Then I realized that I didn't have to give it up, that I can work anywhere. Heck, I could hire a manager to run the bakery here and even open a second location in L.A. Whatever it takes."

"Maybe, but there's nowhere like Emerald Springs. Your bakery belongs here. Our family is here, and this is where I belong, where we belong. Now that I'm back," he said as he took her hand in his and held it lightly. "I'm ready to get started on the rest of our life together. I can't be here without you, knowing you're always so close but not mine."

"So you came back without knowing what would happen?"

"I knew there was no chance of getting you back if I didn't return, so I took the leap, and here I am. I'm all in now, so if you turn me down I don't know what I'm going to do. I flew Chad and Daniel to L.A. for the weekend, and they helped me pack up the condo. It's on the market as we speak." The arrogant, self-assured man who had let her walk away was gone. In his place stood a humbled man, terrified he wouldn't get that second chance he'd gambled on.

"That was fast."

"Hey, when it's right, it's right," he said with a laugh. "I've got stuff in storage both back in L.A. and here, and for now I'm basically living out of a suitcase. Which means I have a lot of work to do, but first ... "

Adam cupped her face in his hands and paused for a second to savor the moment he hoped they'd always remember as the time they realized they'd be together forever. Her blue eyes, fringed with sooty black lashes, gazed up at him, unflinching. Like the last time he'd stormed across a room to kiss her silly, he hoped this time would end up much the same. His voice was low, raspy with emotion. "I'm going to kiss you, unless you tell me not to."

Her eyelids fluttered closed and she snaked her arms around his waist. "What are you waiting for?"

He brushed his lips against hers, softly, until she tightened her grip, her hands splayed against his back. He coaxed her lips open and tasted her, tightening his hold as a soft moan escaped her. She responded by exploring his mouth with equal enthusiasm, pulling herself tighter against him until his mind clouded with hazy desire. He ran his fingers through her hair, wondering how he had ever managed to keep his hands to himself.

Ashley cleared her throat, and they pulled apart from one another, reluctantly. Still gazing into Zoe's eyes like a lovesick teenager, he said, "Sorry, Ashley."

She laughed. "As much as I enjoy this beautiful display of affection, we might have customers come in for their orders."

He took Zoe's hand. "There's something I want to show you."

Chapter Thirteen

Zoe stole glances at Adam as he navigated the car through town, past farms, past fields of tulips and crops, until they reached a residential area. They passed manicured lawns lush with new spring growth as the sweet air flowed through the open car windows and the shouts of children at play drifted on the breeze. They stopped in front of a beautiful, rambling home sitting at the back of a sea of sprawling emerald grass. A blonde woman in a matching royal blue skirt and blazer strode up the walk and entered the house, apparently not bothered by the couple pulling up in front of her house. He put the car in park, turned off the radio, and turned to her, his face serious but hopeful. Her breath caught in her throat, emotion overtaking her. Unbidden, tears sprang to her eyes.

"What's wrong?" He unbuckled his seatbelt and stroked her cheek.

"Nothing. They're happy tears. I just feel so overwhelmed right now. Now that you're here, it just seems unreal. It's a lot to take in."

He laughed and wiped a tear from her cheek with his thumb. "Well, then I hope you brought some tissues because I'm about to lay something on you."

She laughed, relieved he could lighten the situation. "I'll be fine. I don't know why I cry when I'm happy. So go on, tell me, what's the big surprise?"

"Come with me." His eyes glinted with mischief and possibility.

He got out of the car and hurried around to her side to open the door for her, offering her a hand as she pulled herself out. His easy smile was gone, a nervous look replacing it. She stepped onto the sidewalk, the air still clinging to moisture from rain earlier in the day. A light breeze fluttered through the trees that lined the street as she looked up into the eyes of the man she loved. Whatever he said next, this moment was perfect.

Adam took both her hands in his and shifted restlessly . "I want to show you something."

He dropped one of her hands and led her up the path to the door of the house. The woman hadn't looked familiar to her, but maybe Adam knew her. He knocked twice on the front door, then turned the knob and stepped over the threshold without waiting for a response. Thoroughly confused, she followed him in, her fingers still laced between his. He squeezed her hand and led her into the foyer of the beautiful craftsman style home. The gleaming hand-scraped wood floors stretched out before them, leading into oversized rooms that were strangely empty. The woman she'd seen earlier came around the corner, her heels clicking on the tile in the kitchen.

"Adam, how are you?" They shook hands, and Zoe's curiosity grew.

"I'm great, thanks. Zoe, this is Miranda. My real estate agent." Miranda took her hand and shook enthusiastically, oblivious to her confusion.

"Shall I show you around?" Miranda asked. With a hand at the small of her back, solid and reassuring in this odd situation, Adam guided Zoe to follow her..

Miranda led them through the living room, complete with floor-to-ceiling windows that showcased a huge backyard and built-in bookshelves. A stone fireplace rambled from the floor to the ceiling and took up half the wall on one side of the room. They wandered through to the kitchen, where she couldn't help but gasp and stare at the gourmet appliances with wide-eyed appreciation. A double oven and oversized kitchen island pulled her in, and the huge Viking stove top practically advertised all the meals the occupants could cook for friends and family. A cozy dining nook completed the area, and she stopped short of picturing herself serving birthday cake to their future children and a gaggle of their little friends. The rest of the house was just as impressive—one beautiful room after the other, and she worked to keep the hope rising within her from getting out of control. Adam hadn't offered any explanation, and she couldn't let her imagination run away with her.

Finally, they stood in the master bedroom after touring the decadent en suite bathroom. She practically swooned at the creamy ivory marble counters and oversized soaking bathtub, the natural stone shower big enough for two people, and the amazing his and hers closets. Her tidy little apartment over the bakery suddenly felt cramped and plain.

Finally, he spoke. "What do you think?"

"I think it's gorgeous. This might be the nicest house I've ever been in."

"Do you want it?"

She covered her mouth as a loud laugh escaped. "What?" she sputtered, unbelieving, but releasing the tenuous hold she had on her expectations.

"I was going to just go ahead and put in an offer, but I thought you might want to have a say. If you like it, too, we should buy it. And live here. Together." He watched for her reaction.

"Wow. When you make plans, you make plans."

"You're not the only one who doesn't have time to waste," he teased.

She laughed and looked around the room, letting herself imagine waking up there every morning. "Then, yes, I like it. I'd love to live here with you." That was an understatement, but she was finding herself at a loss for words.

"There's one more thing." He pulled a small black velvet box from his pocket, and she was certain all the air had been sucked out of the room. He lowered himself to one knee and flipped the box open with his thumb. "Zoe Miller, I have loved you since

I was a boy. You are everything to me, and I don't want to live another moment without knowing you'll be by my side for the rest of our lives. Will you marry me?"

Through a veil of tears, she looked into his eyes and saw her future. Everything they had gone through in the past was worth the struggle now that they had arrived in this moment. She nodded her assent, unable to form the words to say "yes," and he slid a diamond ring onto her finger. He stood and pulled her into his arms, both of them too overcome to speak. She felt his heartbeat beneath her cheek, and finally, everything was right. Her happy tears soaked the fabric of his shirt, and she wiped them fruitlessly with her fingertips, the room's light catching the diamond's facets.

She nestled closer into his embrace and held her left hand out so she could admire the ring. "It's stunning," she said when she found her voice.

"It was my mother's wedding ring, and I know that she would've wanted you to have it. She loved you." Adam's breath was warm on the top of her head as he spoke. "My dad was saving it for you."

"What?" Her voice was choked with emotion.

"I think he knew things would work out between us before we did, and I know he wouldn't want anyone else to have it. Chad and Daniel agreed, too. You're already a part of the family; this just makes it official."

"I love you." She tilted her head up to face him to find he was already looking down at her, his eyes conveying the emotions she couldn't name.

"I love you, too," he whispered. His lips brushed against hers, gently at first. .

Her body came to life under his touch, the emotions of the day finally finding an outlet. She returned his kiss, and without conscious thought her hands roamed over the firm muscle of his chest and the hard planes of his stomach, his skin warm through his shirt. Her lips moved against his insistently until his mouth opened enough for her to slip her tongue inside. She deepened the kiss, noting with satisfaction how his grip on her back tightened. A low moan grumbled up his throat as he responded to her, their tongues tangling as they enjoyed one another. She smiled through the kiss, knowing that her heart had finally found its home.

The real estate agent's heels clicking against the tile in the kitchen drifted into her consciousness, and she pulled back from him. Her heart was pounding in her chest and her eyes couldn't quite focus; her mind still buzzed with hazy desire and happiness. She cleared her throat and shook her head quickly. Being with Adam made time and place slip away as she surrendered to the feelings he evoked in her. His lips curled into a satisfied smile as he looked down at her. He smoothed a hand over the back of her head, threading his fingers through her hair, and said, "I guess we should go tell her that we'll take it."

• • •

Adam pulled into the parking lot of Emerald Eats, and Zoe paused before unbuckling herself. The Whitmans were waiting inside, likely ready to celebrate their engagement. This was one of those moments she'd always dreamed of. To be here with her future husband, wearing a family wedding ring … . it was finally real. Perfect. He opened her door and took her hand as she stepped out of the car. Without a word, they walked hand in hand into the restaurant.

Conversations stopped when they opened the door, and half the restaurant erupted in applause and cheers when Adam held up her left hand and shouted, "She said yes!"

Ashley wound her way through the tables, smiling from ear to ear, until she reached them and threw her arms around Zoe. "I'm so happy for you!" she squealed, her joy infectious.

Zoe hugged her back and gave herself over to the jubilance bubbling up within her. The man of her dreams had proposed. They were going to live in a gorgeous house, and she was finally going to be a member of the family she loved. What could be better? The trio walked to the back of the restaurant where everyone was waiting for them with huge smiles. The excitement strummed through the air, almost palpable in its intensity. She took a moment to look at everyone around the table, people she had known and loved her whole life, and commit the moment to memory. Richard walked around the table and shook Adam's hand, congratulating him, before pulling her into a fierce hug.

"Welcome to the family, sweetheart." His voice was tender, his eyes shining with unshed tears.

A lump formed in her throat as she looked her future father-in-law in the eye. "Thank you. And thank you for the ring. I'm proud to wear it."

"Sheila would have been so happy for you kids. She always loved you." Richard choked on his last word and squeezed her before letting her go and heading back to his seat beside Patty.

The rest of the family made sure to congratulate Adam and hug Zoe before they sat to order dinner and enjoy a round of the restaurant's signature sparkling green tea drink.

Daniel stood and raised his glass, meeting the eyes of everyone around the table before settling on Adam and Zoe. "I know I speak for everyone when I say how happy we are to welcome you to the family, Zoe. You've always been a Whitman in our hearts, now you'll be one in name as well. Congratulations, Adam. This is the best decision you've made in a long time. Cheers!"

The Whitmans raised their glasses and drank in their honor. Zoe couldn't take her eyes off the faces around the table, knowing she was in the middle of one of those moments she'd remember for the rest of her life. The moment her heart found its home.

A Sneak Peek from Emerald Springs Legacy, Book Two

Colleen's Choice by Holley Trent

Colleen Sanders took a bracing breath before mashing the last few digits of the number she never expected to dial again. Slinking off her seat edge, she took sanctuary beneath her abused cherry desk, gripping the edge of her phone base as she went.

Her father had stripped the carpet from the big office two years past and had never gotten around to replacing it. The staff lingering in the hall could probably hear every blink—every whisper—even through her closed door.

She curled into the corner, drawing her knees up to her chin as her target picked up his extension.

"Greg Quinton."

"Greg. Hi." She swallowed the lump in her throat and lowered her voice to a whisper. "How are you?"

"Great. That you, Colleen? Sounds like your rasp."

"Yeah, it's me."

"Was just thinking about you—talking about you, actually—at the retreat last week. Miss you around here."

She pinched the bridge of her nose between her thumb and forefinger, and mentally berated herself for her lachrymose tendencies as of late. Ball-busting Colleen had never been a crier. She hadn't even cried during that one lacrosse match freshman year when a freak collision resulted in her dislocated shoulder and broken nose, although she had introduced the Emerald Springs residents in attendance to the less refined components of her vocabulary. The official had tossed her a yellow card for that outburst. She'd framed it.

"Miss all of you, too," she confessed.

"Hey, can you speak up? I can hardly hear you."

"No. Listen, do you … " She closed her eyes and willed her churning gut to calm. This was just *Greg*. Out of all the calls she'd had to make in recent weeks, this should have been an easy one. Another deep breath. "Listen, do you have any work for me?"

"Work?"

There was surprise in Greg's voice, and Colleen couldn't tell if it was pleasant or otherwise.

"Yes. Got any design work for me?"

A pause. Greg rustled some papers on his end of the call in Seattle, and there was a thump, followed by a loud, squealing whine.

Colleen yanked the phone back from her ear and held it away until the infernal racket ceased.

Greg came back on the line. "Sorry! Sorry."

Colleen put the phone back against her ear and whispered, "What happened?"

"Got so excited I dropped the phone. We're short some boot designs and have been in a frenzy trying to develop new motifs. I'm pretty sure the timing of your phone call is in direct response to the bargains I made with at least three pagan gods last night."

Her shoulders fell with her relief, and she blew out a breath. "Can you pay me up-front?"

Another pause. "How are things at the farm? Any better?"

"No." Why bother explaining? Greg already knew the dirt.

"Damn. Hey, I'll walk the invoice up to accounting right now. We'll try to get the check cut before FedEx gets here. I'll send you specs as soon as I'm back at my desk."

"Greg, thank you. Really. Thank you. You're getting me out of some serious hot water."

He laughed, and Colleen heard the sound of his heels clacking against the concrete floors at the Markson Outfitters corporate headquarters. Already on the move, Greg was. Colleen had learned a lot about efficiency working under that guy for all those years.

"Pays to have friends in high places, huh?" he asked. "Don't worry about it. You're doing me a massive favor. When you see the deadline, you'll understand."

Colleen laughed, too, and couldn't remember the last time she'd heard that sound coming out of her mouth. Things in her life hadn't been conducive to laughter in the past few months. "Thanks for the warning. I'll look for your email."

"Bye, love."

She put the phone in its base and crawled out from her hidey-hole. No sooner had she'd pulled up to her feet than the phone rang again, the display flashing an interoffice extension. She sighed and set the phone on the desktop before stabbing the speaker button. "Yes, Kate?"

"Colleen, you have some visitors here to see you," her secretary said.

Damn it. Kate had her on speakerphone on her end, too. That meant her dependable assistant had probably already told whoever it was that Colleen was unavailable, but they had insisted on having an audience. She couldn't bluff her way out of this visit as easily as she had with Sam Whitman earlier in the morning. Sam—marketing director at the neighboring Emerald Tea Farm— wasn't there to pay her any money, and she sure as shit didn't owe them any, so in her book, a meeting was unnecessary. Mercenary, true, but she couldn't turn Split Acres Farm around if she was on her ass engaging in idle chitchat all day. As it was, she was already digging the farm out of a grave that was filling in faster than she could shovel clear.

"And who are the visitors?" she asked, rubbing the bridge of her nose again.

"The septic tank contractor has finished his work and wants to talk to you ... and Alan's here."

"Who's Alan?"

Kate had said "Alan" in manner indicating Colleen should already know that. She didn't.

"I … think you should talk to him."

That didn't sound good. Did she owe someone a paycheck and had forgotten?

No, that couldn't be it. She'd been staring over the foreman's shoulder for four weeks, approving every timecard to make sure he didn't let any overtime slip in. She'd issued pay for every single one of those hours.

"Fine. Let me just…" she opened and shut her desk drawer twice "…finish up the filing I'm doing, and I'll be right out."

"Yes, ma'am." Kate clicked off.

"Damn it." The matronly assistant never called Colleen "ma'am" unless the situation required a certain performance. It was their unofficial code word.

Colleen shoved her socked feet into the powder blue floral-print rain boots awaiting her near the door and used the small mirror hung over the file cabinets to smooth the lumps from her hair. If someone suggested she had dressed in the dark that morning, the statement wouldn't have been so far from the truth. Being in a perpetual state of exhaustion, she rarely had her eyes open before arriving at Split Acres Farm's operations office, and Kate had poured that first pot of coffee down her gullet. Further, her lights were on the fritz at the old house. Sometimes they worked, sometimes they didn't, and sometimes she got a shock. Literally.

She looked haggard in that reflection. Until recently, she'd looked her age, maybe a little under it. She got good genes from her mother's side, but from her father's side, she got a major headache in the form of four hundred acres of unprofitable farmland. She was thirty-two but feeling pretty damn close to retirement age. No wonder her mother had always been so tired when Colleen and her brother, Jacob, were growing up. There was just so much to do, and she was doing it with far less staff than her parents ever had.

Oh well. She wasn't trying to win a sash and tiara. She just needed to deal with two visitors as efficiently and painlessly as possible.

She straightened her spine, smoothed her expression into the unreadable blank she always met the public with, and pulled open the door.

Showtime.

She was already talking before she'd cleared the end of the long corridor of mostly empty offices, and had her hand extended for the contractor to shake. "Thanks for coming out so fast, Bart." She caught a glimpse of a tall, dark-haired man lingering near the entryway, but she let him remain in her periphery for the time being. One thing at a time.

Bart switched his clipboard to his left hand and wrapped his big, rough, right hand around hers. "You should have called weeks ago when the plumbing started backing up. Would have been less of a problem."

She was perfectly aware of that. Less of a problem, but no less expensive to fix.

"Everything is in working order, then? Tanks are empty?"

He nodded and handed the clipboard over to her. He crooked his thumb toward the door. "Your custodian here looked it over and said it was fine. Signed off on the work. I just need a check."

All the words made sense. They were English, after all, but they didn't seem to apply to her particular situation. She squared her shoulders and cocked up her favored eyebrow. "I'm sorry?"

Bart took the clipboard back and pointed to something printed in the terms. "Payable upon completion. I guess you don't have a line of credit?"

Her teeth clenched, and she sucked a sobering breath through her nose. *Damn you, Daddy.* She'd waited as long as she did to call them in the first place because she expected to have money to pay the bill in the thirty days it took it to come due. Now she'd have to go rob Peter to pay Paul again.

She took the clipboard back and raised her chin, hoping to garner some sense of authority in the situation, but on the inside she was crumbling. Mess after mess, it never let up. How much more could she take?

"And my *custodian* signed off on it, you said?" She brought the paper up to her eyes and squinted at the scrawled signature. Alan … something-or-other.

Finally, she gave the man more than just her peripheral vision. She stared at him dead-on, expecting him to flinch and blanch like all the others did, but he lifted a hand in greeting and grinned.

Her jaw fell open, and she was stunned momentarily by the blue of his eyes, his chiseled jaw, his dark hair—deliciously unkempt and tickling the top of his collar—and the strong forearms her eyes skimmed down to as he twirled a ratchet wrench between long, tanned fingers.

A stranger, and if she had to guess, her father was to blame for him being there. Why did he agree to let her come home and do the job if he wasn't going to get out of the way to let her do it?

She closed her mouth and swallowed, turning her attention back to Bart. "Have a seat. I'll go cut you a check."

Bart shrugged, shuffled across the worn carpet, and plopped into one of the vinyl chairs near the door.

"Alan," she said, spinning on her boot heel and striding toward the hall. "Why don't you join me in my office and tell me about the work while I run this check through Quickbooks?"

"Yes, certainly, Colleen."

She stumbled a bit over her own feet, glad that no one, beyond the corporate sheltie lounging brazenly in the middle of the hall, could see it. She stepped over the dog and concentrated on her breathing as she approached her office.

Dear lord, he had an accent.

Get a grip, woman.

By the time she plopped her butt in her desk chair and punched her computer monitor button, her supposed custodian joined her in the office, and the blush inching up her neck had receded.

"Close the door, please."

He gave her a speculative look but put his hand on the doorknob and pushed.

She ducked her head behind her computer monitor, clicking her mouse blindly at nothing in particular. She couldn't see straight for some reason, and she didn't think it was low blood sugar

Gorgeous man. Too bad she'd have to fire him.

The Emerald Springs Legacy Series

Follow the Whitman and Sanders families in their continuing saga as they confront old rivalries and discover new love while protecting their legacy at the Emerald Tea Farm. Look for these upcoming installments in this exciting new continuity series from Crimson Romance:

Adam's Ambition by Monica Tillery
Colleen's Choice by Holley Trent
Chad's Chance by Elley Arden
Daniel's Decision by Nicole Flockton
Ashley's Allegiance by Robyn Neeley

To learn more about the Emerald Springs series, visit our website for more details, author interviews, and a special free prequel story.